P9-DFM-324
R00957 95399

8-18-03
3

THE FOLGER LIBRARY
SHAKESPEARE

Designed to make Shakespeare's classic plays available to the general reader, each edition contains a reliable text with modernized spelling and punctuation, scene-by-scene plot summaries, and explanatory notes clarifying obscure and obsolete expressions. An interpretive essay and accounts of Shakespeare's life and theater form an instructive preface to each play.

Louis B. Wright, General Editor, was the Director of the Folger Shakespeare Library from 1948 until his retirement in 1968. He is the author of *Middle-Class Culture in Elizabethan England, Religion and Empire, Shakespeare for Everyman,* and many other books and essays on the history and literature of the Tudor and Stuart periods.

Virginia Lamar, Assistant Editor, served as research assistant to the Director and Executive Secretary of the Folger Shakespeare Library from 1946 until her death in 1968. She is the author of *English Dress in the Age of Shakespeare* and *Travel and Roads in England,* and coeditor of William Strachey's *Historie of Travell into Virginia Britania.*

McKinley Park Branch
1915 West 35th Street
Chicago, Illinois 60609

The Folger Shakespeare Library

The Folger Shakespeare Library in Washington, D.C., a research institute founded and endowed by Henry Clay Folger and administered by the Trustees of Amherst College, contains the world's largest collection of Shakespeareana. Although the Folger Library's primary purpose is to encourage advanced research in history and literature, it has continually exhibited a profound concern in stimulating a popular interest in the Elizabethan period.

GENERAL EDITOR

LOUIS B. WRIGHT

Director, Folger Shakespeare Library, 1948–1968

ASSISTANT EDITOR

VIRGINIA A. LaMAR

Executive Secretary, Folger Shakespeare Library, 1946–1968

TWELFTH NIGHT,

OR

WHAT YOU WILL

by WILLIAM SHAKESPEARE

McKinley Park Branch
1915 West 35th Street
Chicago, Illinois 60609

WSP

WASHINGTON SQUARE PRESS
PUBLISHED BY POCKET BOOKS
New York   London   Toronto   Sydney   Tokyo   Singapore

Most Washington Square Press Books are available at special quantity discounts for bulk purchases for sales promotions, premiums or fund raising. Special books or book excerpts can also be created to fit specific needs.

For details write the office of the Vice President of Special Markets, Pocket Books, 1230 Avenue of the Americas, New York, New York 10020.

A Washington Square Press Publication of
POCKET BOOKS, a division of Simon & Schuster Inc.
1230 Avenue of the Americas, New York, NY 10020

Copyright © 1960 by Simon & Schuster Inc.

All rights reserved, including the right to reproduce
this book or portions thereof in any form whatsoever.
For information address Pocket Books, 1230 Avenue
of the Americas, New York, NY 10020

ISBN: 0-671-72954-3

First Pocket Books printing October 1964

37 36 35 34 33 32 31 30 29 28

WASHINGTON SQUARE PRESS and WSP colophon are
registered trademarks of Simon & Schuster Inc.

Printed in the U.S.A.

Preface

This edition of *Twelfth Night* is designed to make available a readable text of one of Shakespeare's most popular plays. In the centuries since Shakespeare many changes have occurred in the meanings of words, and some clarification of Shakespeare's vocabulary may be helpful. To provide the reader with necessary notes in the most accessible format, we have placed them on the pages facing the text that they explain. We have tried to make these notes as brief and simple as possible. Preliminary to the text we have also included a brief statement of essential information about Shakespeare and his stage. Readers desiring more detailed information should refer to the books suggested in the references, and if still further information is needed, the bibliographies in those books will provide the necessary clues to the literature of the subject.

The early texts of all of Shakespeare's plays provide only inadequate stage directions, and it is conventional for modern editors to add many that clarify the action. Such additions, and additions to entrances, are placed in square brackets.

All illustrations are from material in the Folger Library collections.

L. B. W.
V. A. L.

August 1, 1959

R00957 95399

A Comedy Mad and Merry

With the writing of *Twelfth Night* Shakespeare reached perhaps his highest achievement in sheer comedy, the comedy of merriment and gaiety untinged with any shadow of unhappy implication. Not even Malvolio's undoing is anything more than a practical joke visited upon a pompous official who would be the wiser for the lessons of the jokesters. The efforts of a few actors and critics to portray Malvolio as a figure of sentimental pathos are wasted. He is the butt of a mad jest and well deserves the laughter that his predicament inspires. From first to last, the Comic Spirit hovers over this play and both actors and audience join in the gaiety.

In spirit *Twelfth Night* is a companion piece to *As You Like It*, and its composition appears to have followed closely upon the writing of the latter play. The date that seems most reasonable is some time in 1601. As in *As You Like It*, Shakespeare again demonstrates the confidence and assurance of a mature writer of comedy who understands human nature so profoundly that he can instill a sense of reality into situations that in the hands of a lesser dramatist would have lapsed into romantic absurdity. So skillful is Shakespeare, however, that the audience forgets that the plot turns on an improbable set of coincidences and mistaken identities, devices already well worn when Plautus used them to entertain the Roman spectators who witnessed his *Menaechmi*. But the absurd plot is not the important element in *Twelfth Night;* the important thing is what Shakespeare does with this plot, the way he brings to life a group of unforgettable characters for whom the plot is merely a convenient expedient for displaying their qualities and quirks. We remember *Twelfth Night* for the people whom we encounter in it rather than for the working out of the romantic action of the principals. It is a foregone conclusion when the play opens that the lovesick Orsino, after many a scene of frustration, will win some lady, for that is the way of romantic comedy, but we care little about the denouement of this main plot. Our attention soon centers upon lesser characters in the household of the Lady Olivia and the goings on belowstairs, with drunken Sir Toby, foolish Sir Andrew Aguecheek, and the sprightly and devilish minx Maria.

For zany revelry that the audience is nevertheless willing to accept as within the range of realistic possibility, the theatre has rarely seen the equal of the revel scenes in *Twelfth Night*. At times the action approaches fantasy, but it never goes over the thin line that separates the world of actuality from the realm of comic caprice or slapstick. We always think of Sir Toby or Maria, Sir Andrew or Feste the clown, as definite human beings and not as the conventional automata of farce. Shakespeare made his people live and breathe the air of reality. We have all known some pompous Malvolio who thought there would be no more cakes and ale because he was virtuous. If we do not recognize in Sir Toby the precise counterpart of some ne'er-do-well of our acquaintance, we at least know the type; if Sir Andrew is so completely the quintessence of foolishness that we cannot include him in our known acquaintances, we nevertheless know individuals who have some of the components of his folly; if Maria is a wilder little vixen than most of those we know, we have all encountered her kind. Though Feste the clown may be a little further removed from the common procession who pass daily before our eyes, his witty commentary is the kind that we sometimes discover—and remember—in a new acquaintance. Though characters similar to these are stock parts in comedy, in *Twelfth Night* they achieve a reality that has given them permanence in our memories and our affections.

The occasion on which *Twelfth Night* was first performed is unknown, but Professor Leslie Hotson has published a fascinating book in an attempt to prove that the play was written to order for the festivities in Queen Elizabeth's palace at Whitehall on Twelfth Night, January 6, 1601, when she entertained Virginio Orsino, Duke of Bracciano, an emissary from Italy. The correspondence of the Duke's name with that of the lovesick Duke of Illyria in *Twelfth Night*, the fact that Shakespeare's company was called upon to provide the entertainment at Whitehall on January 6, 1601, and other coincidences, make Mr. Hotson's thesis appealing, but when all the circumstantial evidence is summed up, the case is not made. Furthermore, it is not likely that the portrayal of the Duke of Illyria would have been received as a compliment by the visiting Italian dignitary. One must dismiss Mr. Hotson's theory as ingenious and skillfully reasoned, but not consonant with the verifiable facts.

Although one cannot prove that the play was written to order in eleven days for the particular entertainment at Whitehall in 1601 of the Duke of Bracciano, the tone of the play suggests that Shakespeare may have prepared it with a later court performance in mind. His company was frequently called upon to provide plays at court, and it was always well to have one in store against a command performance. It may be that the visit of Orsino, Duke of Bracciano, with its attendant buzz of gossip, suggested the name of Shakespeare's Duke of Illyria, for after his departure there could be no harm in ringing a faint bell of topicality, a note that might induce a smile from courtiers who recalled the recent visitor. Certainly we know that the play was popular enough to be chosen for a night of revels at the Middle Temple in 1602, for on February 2, 1602, John Manningham wrote in his diary:

At our feast we had a play called *Twelve Night, or What You Will,* much like the *Comedy of Errors,* or *Menaechmi* in Plautus, but most like and near to that in Italian called *Inganni.* A good practice in it to make the

A scene from a version of Plautus' *Menaechmi*.
From Bernardo Dovizi, *La calandra* (1526).

steward believe his lady widow was in love
with him, by counterfeiting a letter as from his
lady in general terms, telling him what she
liked best in him, and prescribing his gesture
in smiling, his apparel, etc., and then when he
came to practice, making him believe they took
him to be mad.

For the members of the Middle Temple at their
annual feast, perhaps for the court of the Queen
herself, *Twelfth Night* was a merry play fit for an
occasion of fun and gaiety.

SOURCE AND STAGE HISTORY

Shakespeare took the main plot of *Twelfth Night*
from a tale, "Of Apolonius and Silla," included in
Barnabe Riche's *Riche His Farewell to Military
Profession* (1581). The story was a popular one
and had been in circulation a long time. A comedy
written in Siena about 1531, *Gl'Ingannati*, used the
theme, and Manningham doubtless meant this play
in his reference in the diary. Matteo Bandello told
the story again in No. 36, Part Two, of his *Novelle*,
and it was translated into French in François de
Belleforest's *Histoires Tragiques*. A Latin play, entitled *Laelia*, translated from *Gl'Ingannati*, was presented in 1595 at Queen's College, Cambridge. Obviously the plot was both familiar and popular. The
subplot concerning Malvolio and the revelers
Shakespeare apparently invented himself, and he

interwove the two elements together so skillfully that the reader gets the illusion of a unity which does not really exist.

Sir Edmund Chambers has suggested that although Shakespeare was too wise a dramatist to meddle in affairs of state, he may have touched on a bit of backstairs gossip in the portrayal of Malvolio. Such allusions would serve to provoke harmless laughter and would not bring either the dramatist or the acting company into jeopardy. The particular gossip that Malvolio's portrayal may have touched concerned Sir William Knollys, Comptroller of the Royal Household, a pompous and unpopular official, whose quarters adjoined those of some of the Queen's maids of honor. The giggling and "frisking" of the girls kept him awake, and he made himself ridiculous trying to curb their gaiety and noise. More than this, though he was married and affected great probity, he secretly pursued Mary Fitton, one of the maids of honor, who led him on for sport, though she was carrying on a serious love affair with the Earl of Pembroke. The character of Malvolio is so like that of Sir William that it is hard to resist the belief that some courtier supplied Shakespeare with the material for a caricature that would have rocked with laughter everyone except Sir William.

Whatever may have been the occasion of the first performance of *Twelfth Night*, it undoubtedly was popular from the beginning, with both the court and the public. In 1618 and 1623, it had revivals at court, and allusions show that the public remembered the play and its characters. When the theatres reopened after the Restoration, *Hamlet* was the first play and *Twelfth Night* was the second by Shakespeare that William D'Avenant chose to produce. Samuel Pepys went to see it but, unlike most other spectators, was not amused. One night in 1661, "walking in Lincoln's Inn Fields," Pepys "observed at the Opera a new play, *Twelfth Night*, was acted, and the King there; so I against my own mind and resolution could not forbear to go in, which did make the play seem a burden to me and I took no pleasure at all in it; and so after it was done went home with my mind troubled for my going thither after my swearing to my wife that I would never go to a play without her." Clearly, the trouble was less with *Twelfth Night* than with Pepys' bad conscience over slipping off from his wife, but he was conditioned against enjoying this play, which he witnessed twice more, in 1663 and 1669. He commented that it was "but a silly play, and not related to the name or day," and finally that it was "one of the weakest plays that ever I saw on the stage." Pepys, however, was voicing a minority opinion, for the play has been almost continually on the stage except for a desolate period in the history of the theatre between 1705 and 1741.

During the nineteenth century, the play was popular on both sides of the Atlantic and was almost constantly on the boards. It has been acted just as Shakespeare wrote it and also in a variety of

adaptations including operatic versions. An opera-
like adaptation made by the actor-producer Frederic
Reynolds in 1820 enjoyed considerable popularity.
Actors and actresses have liked the play because it
gives an opportunity for many good roles and is
not dominated by any single star. Viola and Malvolio are probably the roles most favored by the
acting profession, but Sir Toby, Sir Andrew, Maria,
and Feste are parts in which actors have made notable reputations. During 1958 and 1959, the Old
Vic Company of London performed a particularly
effective *Twelfth Night,* in which Dudley Jones,
playing Feste, gave such an able portrayal of the
clown's role that he almost stole the show.

Few plays in the history of English drama have
enjoyed such continuous popularity. Through the
centuries the silvery laughter of high comedy has
hung over this play, and almost every epoch has
found it amusing. Its humor is timeless, as the best
humor must be, and it does not depend for its ef-
fects upon ephemeral allusions or the brittle play of
wit exemplified by the wisecracks of current television "comedy." Its humor is as profound as human nature, which Shakespeare comprehended
with a depth of sympathy and understanding that
has been vouchsafed few other dramatists.

THE TEXT

The textual problems of *Twelfth Night* are un-
complicated. No printing occurred before the First

Folio of 1623, and that text has fewer errors than most of the plays. It contains stage directions and indications for music that suggest that the Folio version may have been printed from a good prompt copy. All later versions of the play, of course, are based on the First Folio.

THE AUTHOR

As early as 1598 Shakespeare was so well known as a literary and dramatic craftsman that Francis Meres, in his *Palladis Tamia: Wits Treasury*, referred in flattering terms to him as "mellifluous and honey-tongued Shakespeare," famous for his *Venus and Adonis*, his *Lucrece*, and "his sugared sonnets," which were circulating "among his private friends." Meres observes further that "as Plautus and Seneca are accounted the best for comedy and tragedy among the Latins, so Shakespeare among the English is the most excellent in both kinds for the stage," and he mentions a dozen plays that had made a name for Shakespeare. He concludes with the remark "that the Muses would speak with Shakespeare's fine filed phrase if they would speak English."

To those acquainted with the history of the Elizabethan and Jacobean periods, it is incredible that anyone should be so naïve or ignorant as to doubt the reality of Shakespeare as the author of the plays that bear his name. Yet so much nonsense has been written about other "candidates" for the plays that it is well to remind readers that no credible evidence that would stand up in a court of law has ever been adduced to prove either that Shakespeare did not write his plays or that anyone else wrote them. All the theories offered for the authorship of Francis Bacon, the Earl of Derby, the Earl of Oxford, the Earl of Hertford, Christopher Marlowe, and a score of other candidates are mere conjectures spun from the active imaginations of persons who confuse hypothesis and conjecture with evidence.

As Meres' statement of 1598 indicates, Shakespeare was already a popular playwright whose name carried weight at the box office. The obvious reputation of Shakespeare as early as 1598 makes the effort to prove him a myth one of the most absurd in the history of human perversity.

The anti-Shakespeareans talk darkly about a plot of vested interests to maintain the authorship of Shakespeare. Nobody has any vested interest in Shakespeare, but every scholar is interested in the truth and in the quality of evidence advanced by special pleaders who set forth hypotheses in place of facts.

The anti-Shakespeareans base their arguments upon a few simple premises, all of them false. These false premises are that Shakespeare was an unlettered yokel without any schooling, that nothing is known about Shakespeare, and that only a noble lord or the equivalent in background could have written the plays. The facts are that more is known about Shakespeare than about most dramatists of his day, that he had a very good education, acquired in the Stratford Grammar School, that the plays show no evidence of profound book learning, and that the knowledge of kings and courts evident in the plays is no greater than any intelligent young man could have picked up at second hand. Most anti-Shakespeareans are naïve and betray an obvious snobbery. The author of their favorite plays, they imply, must have had a college diploma framed and hung on his study wall like the one in their dentist's office, and obviously so great a writer must have had a title or some equally significant evidence of exalted social background. They forget that genius has a way of cropping up in unexpected places and that none of the great creative writers of the world got his inspiration in a college or university course.

William Shakespeare was the son of John Shakespeare of Stratford-upon-Avon, a substantial citizen of that small but busy market town in the center of the rich agricultural county of Warwick. John Shakespeare kept a shop, what we would call a general store; he dealt in wool and other produce and gradually acquired property. As a youth, John Shakespeare had learned the trade of glover and leather worker. There is no contemporary evidence that the elder Shakespeare was a butcher, though the anti-Shakespeareans like to talk about the ignorant "butcher's boy of Stratford." Their only evidence is a statement by gossipy John Aubrey, more than a century after William Shakespeare's birth, that young William followed his father's trade, and when he killed a calf, "he would do it in a high style and make a speech." We would like to believe the story true, but Aubrey is not a very credible witness.

John Shakespeare probably continued to operate a farm at Snitterfield that his father had leased. He married Mary Arden, daughter of his father's landlord, a man of some property. The third of their eight children was William, baptized on April 26, 1564, and probably born three days before. At least, it is conventional to celebrate April 23 as his birthday.

The Stratford records give considerable information about John Shakespeare. We know that he held several municipal offices including those of alderman and mayor. In 1580 he was in some sort of legal difficulty and was fined for neglecting a summons of the Court of Queen's Bench requiring him to appear at Westminster and be bound over to keep the peace.

As a citizen and alderman of Stratford, John Shakespeare was entitled to send his son to the grammar school free. Though the records are lost, there can be no reason to doubt that this is where young William received his education. As any student of the period knows, the grammar schools provided the basic education in Latin learning and literature. The Elizabethan grammar school is not to be confused with modern grammar schools. Many cultivated men of the day received all their formal education in the grammar schools. At the universities in this period a student would have received little training that would have inspired him to be a creative writer. At Stratford young Shakespeare would have acquired a familiarity with Latin and some little knowledge of Greek. He would have read Latin authors and become acquainted with the plays of Plautus and Terence. Undoubtedly, in this period of his life he received that stimulation to read and explore for himself the world of ancient and modern history which he later utilized in his plays. The youngster who does not acquire this type of intellectual curiosity *before* college days rarely develops as a result of a college course the kind of mind Shakespeare demonstrated. His learning in books was anything but profound, but he clearly had the probing curiosity that sent him in search of information, and he had a keenness in the observation of nature and of humankind that finds reflection in his poetry.

There is little documentation for Shakespeare's boyhood. There is little reason why there should be. Nobody knew that he was going to be a dramatist about whom any scrap of information would be prized in the centuries to come. He was merely an active and vigorous youth of Stratford, perhaps assisting his father in his business, and no Boswell bothered to write down facts about him. The most important record that we have is a marriage license issued by the Bishop of Worcester on November

28, 1582, to permit William Shakespeare to marry Anne Hathaway, seven or eight years his senior; furthermore, the Bishop permitted the marriage after reading the banns only once instead of three times, evidence of the desire for haste. The need was explained on May 26, 1583, when the christening of Susanna, daughter of William and Anne Shakespeare, was recorded at Stratford. Two years later, on February 2, 1585, the records show the birth of twins to the Shakespeares, a boy and a girl who were christened Hamnet and Judith.

What William Shakespeare was doing in Stratford during the early years of his married life, or when he went to London, we do not know. It has been conjectured that he tried his hand at schoolteaching, but that is a mere guess. There is a legend that he left Stratford to escape a charge of poaching in the park of Sir Thomas Lucy of Charlecote, but there is no proof of this. There is also a legend that when first he came to London, he earned his living by holding horses outside a playhouse and presently was given employment inside, but there is nothing better than eighteenth-century hearsay for this. How Shakespeare broke into the London theatres as a dramatist and actor we do not know. But lack of information is not surprising, for Elizabethans did not write their autobiographies, and we know even less about the lives of many writers and some men of affairs than we know about Shakespeare. By 1592 he was so well established and popular that he incurred the envy of the dramatist and pamphleteer Robert Greene, who referred to him as an "upstart crow . . . in his own conceit the only Shake-scene in a country." From this time onward, contemporary allusions and references in legal documents enable the scholar to chart Shakespeare's career with greater accuracy than is possible with most other Elizabethan dramatists.

By 1594 Shakespeare was a member of the company of actors known as the Lord Chamberlain's Men. After the accession of James I, in 1603, the company would have the sovereign for their patron and would be known as the King's Men. During the period of its greatest prosperity, this company would have as its principal theatres the Globe and the Blackfriars. Shakespeare was both an actor and a shareholder in the company. Tradition has assigned him such acting roles as Adam in *As You Like It* and the Ghost in *Hamlet*, a modest place on the stage that suggests that he may have had other duties in the management of the company. Such conclusions, however, are based on surmise.

What we do know is that his plays were popular and that he was highly successful in his vocation. His first play may have been *The Comedy of Errors*, acted perhaps in 1591. Certainly this was one of his earliest plays. The three parts of *Henry VI* were acted sometime between 1590 and 1592. Critics are not in agreement about precisely how much Shakespeare wrote of these three plays. *Richard III* probably dates from 1593. With this play Shakespeare captured the imagination of Elizabethan audiences, then enormously interested in historical plays. With *Richard III* Shakespeare also gave an interpretation pleasing to the Tudors of the rise to power of the grandfather of Queen Elizabeth. From this time onward, Shakespeare's plays followed on the stage in rapid succession: *Titus Andronicus, The Taming of the Shrew, The Two Gentlemen of Verona, Love's Labour's Lost, Romeo and Juliet, Richard II, A Midsummer Night's Dream, King John, The Merchant of Venice, Henry IV (Parts I and II), Much Ado About Nothing, Henry V, Julius Cæsar, As You Like It, Twelfth Night, Hamlet, The Merry Wives of Windsor, All's Well That Ends Well, Measure for Measure, Othello, King Lear*, and nine others that followed before Shakespeare retired completely, about 1613.

In the course of his career in London, he made enough money to enable him to retire to Stratford with a competence. His purchase on May 4, 1597, of New Place, then the second-largest dwelling in Stratford, a "pretty house of brick and timber," with a handsome garden, indicates his increasing prosperity. There his wife and children lived while he busied himself in the London theatres. The summer before he acquired New Place, his life was darkened by the death of his only son, Hamnet, a child of eleven. In May, 1602, Shakespeare purchased one hundred and seven acres of fertile farmland near Stratford and a few months later bought a cottage and garden across the alley from New Place. About 1611, he seems to have returned permanently to Stratford, for the next year a legal document refers to him as "William Shakespeare of Stratford-upon-Avon . . . gentleman." To achieve the desired appellation of gentleman, William Shakespeare had seen to it that the College of Heralds in 1596 granted his father a coat of arms. In one step he thus became a second-generation gentleman.

Shakespeare's daughter Susanna made a good match in 1607 with Dr. John Hall, a prominent and prosperous Stratford physician. His second daughter, Judith, did not marry until she was thirty-two years old, and then, under somewhat scandalous circumstances, she married Thomas Quiney, a Stratford vintner. On March 25, 1616, Shakespeare made his will, bequeathing his landed property to Susanna, £300 to Judith, certain sums to other relatives, and his second-best bed to his wife, Anne. Much has been made of the second-best bed, but the legacy probably indicates only that Anne liked that particular bed. Shakespeare, following the practice of the time, may have already arranged with Susanna for his wife's care. Finally, on April 23, 1616, the anniversary of his birth, William Shakespeare died, and he was buried on April 25 within the chancel of Trinity Church, as befitted an honored citizen. On August 6, 1623, a few months before the publication of the collected edition of Shakespeare's plays, Anne Shakespeare joined her husband in death.

During his lifetime Shakespeare made no effort to publish any of his plays, though eighteen appeared in print in single-play editions known as quartos. Some of these are corrupt versions known as "bad quartos." No quarto, so far as is known, had the author's approval. Plays were not considered "literature" any more than most radio and television scripts today are considered literature. Dramatists sold their plays outright to the theatrical companies and it was usually considered in the company's interest to keep plays from getting into print. To achieve a reputation as a man of letters, Shakespeare wrote his *Sonnets* and his narrative poems, *Venus and Adonis* and *The Rape of Lucrece*, but he probably never dreamed that his plays would establish his reputation as a literary genius. Only Ben Jonson, a man known for his colossal conceit, had the crust to call his plays *Works*, as he did when he published an edition in 1616. But men laughed at Ben Jonson.

After Shakespeare's death, two of his old colleagues in the King's Men, John Heminges and Henry Condell, decided that it would be a good thing to print, in more accurate versions than were then available, the plays already published and eighteen additional plays not previously published in quarto. In 1623 appeared *Mr. William Shakespeares Comedies, Histories, & Tragedies. Published according to the True Originall Copies. London. Printed by Isaac Iaggard and Ed. Blount.* This was the famous First Folio, a work that had the authority of Shakespeare's associates. The only play commonly attributed to Shakespeare that was omitted in the First Folio was *Pericles.* In their preface, "To the great Variety of Readers," Heminges and Condell state that whereas "you were abused with diverse stolen and surreptitious copies, maimed and deformed by the frauds and stealths of injurious impostors that exposed them, even those are now offered to your view cured and perfect of their limbs; and all the rest, absolute in their numbers, as he conceived them." What they used for printer's copy is one of the vexed problems of scholarship, and skilled bibliographers have devoted years of study to the question of the relation of the "copy" for the First Folio to Shakespeare's manuscripts. In some cases it is clear that the editors corrected printed quarto versions of the plays, probably by comparison with playhouse scripts. Whether these scripts were in Shakespeare's autograph is anybody's guess. No manuscript of any play in Shakespeare's handwriting has survived. Indeed, very few play manuscripts from this period by any author are extant. The Tudor and Stuart periods had not yet learned to prize autographs and authors' original manuscripts.

Since the First Folio contains eighteen plays not previously printed, it is the only source for these.

For the other eighteen, which had appeared in quarto versions, the First Folio also has the authority of an edition prepared and overseen by Shakespeare's colleagues and professional associates. But since editorial standards in 1623 were far from strict, and Heminges and Condell were actors rather than editors by profession, the texts are sometimes careless. The printing and proofreading of the First Folio also left much to be desired, and some garbled passages have to be corrected and emended. The "good quarto" texts have to be taken into account in preparing a modern edition.

Because of the great popularity of Shakespeare through the centuries, the First Folio has become a prized book, but it is not a very rare one, for it is estimated that 238 copies are extant. The Folger Shakespeare Library in Washington, D.C., has seventy-nine copies of the First Folio, collected by the founder, Henry Clay Folger, who believed that a collation of as many texts as possible would reveal significant facts about the text of Shakespeare's plays. Dr. Charlton Hinman, using an ingenious machine of his own invention for mechanical collating, has made many discoveries that throw light on Shakespeare's text and on printing practices of the day.

The probability is that the First Folio of 1623 had an edition of between 1,000 and 1,250 copies. It is believed that it sold for £1, which made it an expensive book, for £1 in 1623 was equivalent to something between $40 and $50 in modern purchasing power.

During the seventeenth century, Shakespeare was sufficiently popular to warrant three later editions in folio size, the Second Folio of 1632, the Third Folio of 1663–1664, and the Fourth Folio of 1685. The Third Folio added six other plays ascribed to Shakespeare, but these are apocryphal.

THE SHAKESPEAREAN THEATRE

The theatres in which Shakespeare's plays were performed were vastly different from those we know today. The stage was a platform that jutted out into the area now occupied by the first rows of seats on the main floor, what is called the "orchestra" in America and the "pit" in England. This platform had no curtain to come down at the ends of acts and scenes. And although simple stage properties were available, the Elizabethan theatre lacked both the machinery and the elaborate movable scenery of the modern theatre. In the rear of the platform stage was a curtained area that could be used as an inner room, a tomb, or any such scene that might be required. A balcony above this inner room, and perhaps balconies on the sides of the stage, could represent the upper deck of a ship, the entry to Juliet's room, or a prison window. A trap door in the stage provided an entrance for ghosts and devils from the nether regions, and a similar trap in the canopied structure over the stage, known as the "heavens," made it possible to let down angels on a rope. These primitive stage arrangements help to account for many elements in Elizabethan plays. For example, since there was no curtain, the dramatist frequently felt the necessity of writing into his play action to clear the stage at the ends of acts and scenes. The funeral march at the end of *Hamlet* is not there merely for atmosphere; Shakespeare had to get the corpses off the stage. The lack of scenery also freed the dramatist from undue concern about the exact location of his sets, and the physical relation of his various settings to each other did not have to be worked out with the same precision as in the modern theatre.

Before London had buildings designed exclusively for theatrical entertainment, plays were given in inns and taverns. The characteristic inn of the period had an inner courtyard with rooms opening onto balconies overlooking the yard. Players could set up their temporary stages at one end of the yard and audiences could find seats on the balconies out of the weather. The poorer sort could stand or sit on the cobblestones in the yard, which was open to the sky. The first theatres followed this construction, and throughout the Elizabethan period the large public theatres had a yard in front of the stage open to the weather, with two or three tiers of covered balconies extending around the theatre. This physical structure again influenced the writing of plays. Because a dramatist wanted the actors to be heard, he frequently wrote into his play orations that could be delivered with declamatory effect. He also provided spectacle, buffoonery, and broad jests to keep the riotous groundlings in the yard entertained and quiet.

In another respect the Elizabethan theatre differed greatly from ours. It had no actresses. All women's roles were taken by boys, sometimes recruited from the boys' choirs of the London churches. Some of these youths acted their roles with great skill and the Elizabethans did not seem to be aware of any incongruity. The first actresses on the professional English stage appeared after the Restoration of Charles II, in 1660, when exiled Englishmen brought back from France practices of the French stage.

London in the Elizabethan period, as now, was the center of theatrical interest, though wandering actors from time to time traveled through the country performing in inns, halls, and the houses of the nobility. The first professional playhouse, called simply The Theatre, was erected by James Burbage, father of Shakespeare's colleague Richard Burbage, in 1576 on lands of the old Holywell Priory adjacent to Finsbury Fields, a playground and park area just north of the city walls. It had the advantage of being outside the city's jurisdiction and yet was near enough to be easily accessible. Soon after The Theatre was opened, another playhouse called The

Curtain was erected in the same neighborhood. Both of these playhouses had open courtyards and were probably polygonal in shape.

About the time The Curtain opened, Richard Farrant, Master of the Children of the Chapel Royal at Windsor and of St. Paul's, conceived the idea of opening a "private" theatre in the old monastery buildings of the Blackfriars, not far from St. Paul's Cathedral in the heart of the city. This theatre was ostensibly to train the choirboys in plays for presentation at Court, but Farrant managed to present plays to paying audiences and achieved considerable success until aristocratic neighbors complained and had the theatre closed. This first Blackfriars Theatre was significant, however, because it popularized the boy actors in a professional way and it paved the way for a second theatre in the Blackfriars, which Shakespeare's company took over more than thirty years later. By the last years of the sixteenth century, London had at least six professional theatres and still others were erected during the reign of James I.

The Globe Theatre, the playhouse that most people connect with Shakespeare, was erected early in 1599 on the Bankside, the area across the Thames from the city. Its construction had a dramatic beginning, for on the night of December 28, 1598, James Burbage's sons, Cuthbert and Richard, gathered together a crew who tore down the old theatre in Holywell and carted the timbers across the river to a site that they had chosen for a new play-

The Globe Playhouse.
From Visscher's *View of London* (1616).

house. The reason for this clandestine operation was a row with the landowner over the lease to the Holywell property. The site chosen for the Globe was another playground outside of the city's jurisdiction, a region of somewhat unsavory character. Not far away was the Bear Garden, an amphitheatre devoted to the baiting of bears and bulls. This was also the region occupied by many houses of ill fame licensed by the Bishop of Winchester and the source of substantial revenue to him. But it was easily accessible either from London Bridge or by means of the cheap boats operated by the London watermen, and it had the great advantage of being beyond the authority of the Puritanical aldermen of London, who frowned on plays because they lured apprentices from work, filled their heads with improper ideas, and generally exerted a bad influence. The aldermen also complained that the crowds drawn together in the theatre helped to spread the plague.

The Globe was the handsomest theatre up to its time. It was a large building, apparently octagonal in shape and open like its predecessors to the sky in the center, but capable of seating a large audience in its covered balconies. To erect and operate the Globe, the Burbages organized a syndicate composed of the leading members of the dramatic company, of which Shakespeare was a member. Since it was open to the weather and depended on natural light, plays had to be given in the after-

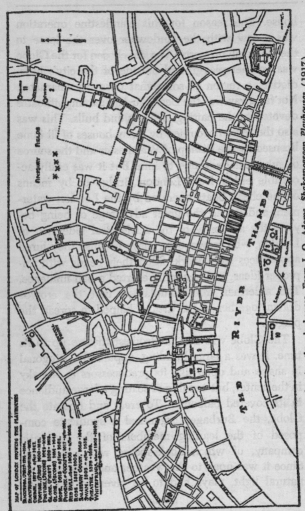

Map of London showing the playhouses. From J. Q. Adams, *Shakespearean Playhouses* (1917).

noon. This caused no hardship in the long afternoons of an English summer, but in the winter the weather was a great handicap and discouraged all except the hardiest. For that reason, in 1608 Shakespeare's company was glad to take over the lease of the second Blackfriars Theatre, a substantial, roomy hall reconstructed within the framework of the old monastery building. This theatre was protected from the weather and its stage was artificially lighted by chandeliers of candles. This became the winter playhouse for Shakespeare's company and at once proved so popular that the congestion of traffic created an embarrassing problem. Stringent regulations had to be made for the movement of coaches in the vicinity. Shakespeare's company continued to use the Globe during the summer months. In 1613 a squib fired from a cannon during a performance of *Henry VIII* fell on the thatched roof and the Globe burned to the ground. The next year it was rebuilt.

London had other famous theatres. The Rose, just west of the Globe, was built by Philip Henslowe, a semiliterate denizen of the Bankside, who

---

Key to playhouses shown on map at left: 1. Blackfriars (First: 1576-1584; Second: 1596-1655); 2. Curtain (1577-after 1627); 3. Fortune (First: 1600-1621; Second: 1623-1661); 4. Globe (First: 1599-1613; Second: 1614-1645); 5. Hope (1613-after 1682); 6. Phoenix or Cockpit (1617-after 1664); 7. Red Bull (about 1605-after 1663); 8. Rose (1587-1605); 9. Salisbury Court (1629-1666); 10. Swan (1595-after 1632); 11. Theatre (1576-1598); 12. Whitefriars (about 1605-1614 [?]).

became one of the most important theatrical owners and producers of the Tudor and Stuart periods. What is more important for historians, he kept a detailed account book, which provides much of our information about theatrical history in his time. Another famous theatre on the Bankside was the Swan, which a Dutch priest, Johannes de Witt, visited in 1596. The crude drawing of the stage which he made was copied by his friend Arend van Buchell; it is one of the important pieces of contemporary evidence for theatrical construction. Among the other theatres, the Fortune, north of the city, on Golding Lane, and the Red Bull, even farther away from the city, off St. John's Street, were the most popular. The Red Bull, much frequented by apprentices, favored sensational and sometimes rowdy plays.

The actors who kept all of these theatres going were organized into companies under the protection of some noble patron. Traditionally actors had enjoyed a low reputation. In some of the ordinances they were classed as vagrants; in the phraseology of the time, "rogues, vagabonds, sturdy beggars, and common players" were all listed together as undesirables. To escape penalties often meted out to these characters, organized groups of actors managed to gain the protection of various personages of high degree. In the later years of Elizabeth's reign, a group flourished under the name of the Queen's Men; another group had the protection of the Lord Admiral and were known as the Lord Admiral's Men. Edward Alleyn, son-in-law of Philip Henslowe, was the leading spirit in the Lord Admiral's Men. Besides the adult companies, troupes of boy actors from time to time also enjoyed considerable popularity. Among these were the Children of Paul's and the Children of the Chapel Royal.

The company with which Shakespeare had a long association had for its first patron Henry Carey, Lord Hunsdon, the Lord Chamberlain, and hence they were known as the Lord Chamberlain's Men. After the accession of James I, they became the King's Men. This company was the great rival of the Lord Admiral's Men, managed by Henslowe and Alleyn.

All was not easy for the players in Shakespeare's time, for the aldermen of London were always eager for an excuse to close up the Blackfriars and any other theatres in their jurisdiction. The theatres outside the jurisdiction of London were not immune from interference, for they might be shut up by order of the Privy Council for meddling in politics or for various other offenses, or they might be closed in time of plague lest they spread infection. During plague times, the actors usually went on tour and played the provinces wherever they could find an audience. Particularly frightening were the plagues of 1592–1594 and 1613 when the theatres closed and the players, like many other Londoners, had to take to the country.

Though players had a low social status, they enjoyed great popularity, and one of the favorite forms of entertainment at Court was the performance of plays. To be commanded to perform at Court conferred great prestige upon a company of players, and printers frequently noted that fact when they published plays. Several of Shakespeare's plays were performed before the sovereign, and Shakespeare himself undoubtedly acted in some of these plays.

REFERENCES FOR FURTHER READING

Many readers will want suggestions for further reading about Shakespeare and his times. The literature in this field is enormous but a few references will serve as guides to further study. A simple and useful little book is Gerald Sanders, *A Shakespeare Primer* (New York, 1950). *A Companion to Shakespeare Studies*, edited by Harley Granville-Barker and G. B. Harrison (Cambridge, Eng., 1934) is a valuable guide. More detailed but still not too voluminous to be confusing is Hazelton Spencer, *The Art and Life of William Shakespeare* (New York, 1940) which, like Sanders' handbook, contains a brief annotated list of useful books on various aspects of the subject. The most detailed and scholarly work providing complete factual information about Shakespeare is Sir Edmund Chambers, *William Shakespeare: A Study of Facts and Problems* (2 vols., Oxford, 1930). For detailed, factual information about the Elizabethan and seventeenth-century stages, the definitive reference works are Sir Edmund Chambers, *The Elizabethan Stage* (4 vols., Oxford, 1923) and Gerald E. Bentley, *The Jacobean and Caroline Stage* (5 vols., Oxford, 1941–1956). Alfred Harbage, *Shakespeare's Audience* (New York, 1941) throws light on the nature and tastes of the customers for whom Elizabethan dramatists wrote.

Although specialists disagree about details of stage construction, the reader will find essential information in John C. Adams, *The Globe Playhouse: Its Design and Equipment* (Barnes & Noble, 1961). A model of the Globe playhouse by Dr. Adams is on permanent exhibition in the Folger Shakespeare Library in Washington, D.C. An excellent description of the architecture of the Globe is Irwin Smith, *Shakespeare's Globe Playhouse: A Modern Reconstruction in Text and Scale Drawings Based upon the Reconstruction of the Globe by John Cranford Adams* (New York, 1956). Another recent study of the physical characteristics of the Globe is C. Walter Hodges, *The Globe Restored* (London, 1953). An easily read history of the early theatres is J. Q. Adams, *Shakespearean Playhouses: A History of English Theatres from the Beginnings to the Restoration* (Boston, 1917).

The following titles on theatrical history will provide information about Shakespeare's plays in later periods: Alfred Harbage, *Theatre for Shakespeare*

(Toronto, 1955); Esther Cloudman Dunn, *Shakespeare in America* (New York, 1939); George C. D. Odell, *Shakespeare from Betterton to Irving* (2 vols., London, 1921); Arthur Colby Sprague, *Shakespeare and the Actors: The Stage Business in His Plays (1660–1905)* (Cambridge, Mass., 1944) and *Shakespearian Players and Performances* (Cambridge, Mass., 1953); Leslie Hotson, *The Commonwealth and Restoration Stage* (Cambridge, Mass., 1928); Alwin Thaler, *Shakspere to Sheridan: A Book About the Theatre of Yesterday and To-day* (Cambridge, Mass., 1922); Ernest Bradlee Watson, *Sheridan to Robertson: A Study of the 19th-Century London Stage* (Cambridge, Mass., 1926). Enid Welsford, *The Court Masque* (Cambridge, Mass., 1927) is an excellent study of the characteristics of this form of entertainment.

The question of the authenticity of Shakespeare's plays arouses perennial attention. A book that demolishes the notion of hidden cryptograms in the plays is William F. Friedman and Elizebeth S. Friedman, *The Shakespearean Ciphers Examined* (New York, 1957). A succinct account of the various absurdities advanced to suggest the authorship of a multitude of candidates other than Shakespeare will be found in R. C. Churchill, *Shakespeare and His Betters* (Bloomington, Ind., 1959) and Frank W. Wadsworth, *The Poacher from Stratford: A Partial Account of the Controversy over the Authorship of Shakespeare's Plays* (Berkeley, Calif., 1958). An essay on the curious notions in the writings of the anti-Shakespeareans is that by Louis B. Wright, "The Anti-Shakespeare Industry and the Growth of Cults," *The Virginia Quarterly Review*, XXXV (1959), 289–303.

Leslie Hotson's ingenious and readable book is entitled *The First Night of Twelfth Night* (New York, 1954). Much information about contemporary conditions surrounding the writing and performance of the play will be found in John W. Draper, *The "Twelfth Night" of Shakespeare's Audience* (Stanford, Calif., 1950). Sir Edmund Chambers, *Shakespeare: A Survey* (London, 1925) contains an essay on *Twelfth Night* in which he mentions the possibility of Sir William Knollys' identification with Malvolio. More information about Knollys will be found in Lady Anne Newdigate-Newdegate, *Gossip from a Muniment Room* (London, 1897). A stimulating discussion of the play will also be found in C. L. Barber, *Shakespeare's Festive Comedy* (Princeton, 1959).

Harley Granville-Barker, *Prefaces to Shakespeare* (5 vols., London, 1927-1948) provides stimulating critical discussion of the plays. An older classic of criticism is Andrew C. Bradley, *Shakespearean Tragedy: Lectures on Hamlet, Othello, King Lear, Macbeth* (London, 1904), which is now available in an inexpensive reprint (New York, 1955). Thomas M. Parrott, *Shakespearean Comedy* (New York, 1949) is scholarly and readable. Shakespeare's dramatizations of English history are examined in E. M. W. Tillyard, *Shakespeare's History*

Plays (London, 1948), and Lily Bess Campbell, *Shakespeare's "Histories," Mirrors of Elizabethan Policy* (San Marino, Calif., 1947) contains a more technical discussion of the same subject.

Reprints of some of the sources for Shakespeare's plays, including *Twelfth Night,* can be found in *Shakespeare's Library* (2 vols., 1850), edited by John Payne Collier, and *The Shakespeare Classics* (12 vols., 1907-1926), edited by Israel Gollancz. Geoffrey Bullough, *Narrative and Dramatic Sources of Shakespeare* (New York, 1957) is the first of a new series of volumes reprinting the sources. For discussion of Shakespeare's use of his sources, see Kenneth Muir, *Shakespeare's Sources: Comedies and Tragedies* (London, 1957). Thomas M. Cranfill has recently edited a facsimile reprint of *Riche His Farewell to Military Profession* (1581), which contains stories that Shakespeare probably drew on for several of his plays, including "Of Apolonius and Silla" used for *Twelfth Night.*

Interesting pictures as well as new information about Shakespeare will be found in F. E. Halliday, *Shakespeare, a Pictorial Biography* (London, 1956). Allardyce Nicoll, *The Elizabethans* (Cambridge, Eng., 1957) contains a variety of illustrations.

A brief, clear, and accurate account of Tudor history is S. T. Bindoff, *The Tudors,* in the Penguin series. A readable general history is G. M. Trevelyan, *The History of England,* first published in 1926 and available in many editions. G. M. Trevelyan, *English Social History,* first published in

1942 and also available in many editions, provides fascinating information about England in all periods. Sir John Neale, *Queen Elizabeth* (London, 1934) is the best study of the great Queen. Various aspects of life in the Elizabethan period are treated in Louis B. Wright, *Middle-Class Culture in Elizabethan England* (Chapel Hill, N.C., 1935; reprinted by Cornell University Press, 1958). *Shakespeare's England: An Account of the Life and Manners of His Age*, edited by Sidney Lee and C. T. Onions (2 vols., Oxford, 1916), provides a large amount of information on many aspects of life in the Elizabethan period. Additional information will be found in Muriel St. C. Byrne, *Elizabethan Life in Town and Country* (Barnes & Noble, 1961).

The Folger Shakespeare Library is currently publishing a series of illustrated pamphlets on various aspects of English life in the sixteenth and seventeenth centuries. The following titles are available: Dorothy E. Mason, *Music in Elizabethan England;* Craig R. Thompson, *The English Church in the Sixteenth Century;* Louis B. Wright, *Shakespeare's Theatre and the Dramatic Tradition;* Giles E. Dawson, *The Life of William Shakespeare;* Virginia A. LaMar, *English Dress in the Age of Shakespeare;* Craig R. Thompson, *The Bible in English, 1525-1611;* Craig R. Thompson, *Schools in Tudor England;* Craig R. Thompson, *Universities in Tudor England;* Lilly C. Stone, *English Sports and Recreations;* Conyers Read, *The Government of England Under Elizabeth.*

[Dramatis Personae.

Orsino, Duke of Illyria.
Sebastian, brother to Viola.
Antonio, a sea captain, friend to Sebastian.
A Sea Captain, friend to Viola.
Valentine,⎫
Curio,⎭ gentlemen attending the Duke.
Sir Toby Belch, uncle to Olivia.
Sir Andrew Aguecheek.
Malvolio, steward to Olivia.
Fabian,⎫
Feste, a Clown,⎭ servants to Olivia.

Olivia, a countess.
Viola, sister to Sebastian.
Maria, attendant to Olivia.

Lords, a Priest, Sailors, Officers, Musicians, and
    Attendants.

SCENE: *A city in Illyria, and the nearby seacoast.*]

TWELFTH NIGHT

ACT I

I. i. Duke Orsino of Illyria is introduced, sighing for love of the Lady Olivia, who denies his suit because she has vowed to forswear the company of men until she has mourned seven •years for her brother's death.

4. **fall:** cadence.

5-7. **it came o'er my ear like the sweet sound/ That breathes upon a bank of violets,/ Stealing and giving odor:** it struck my ear like the sweet sound of a zephyr which, having blown over a bank of violets, has stolen some of their scent and now breathes it forth here.

9. **quick and fresh:** speedily responsive.

10-1. **thy capacity/ Receiveth as the sea:** i.e., your capacity is as boundless as the sea.

12. **validity:** value; **pitch:** synonymous with validity.

13. **falls into abatement and low price:** depreciates in value.

14. **Even:** exactly; **shapes:** images of all kinds; **fancy:** often used for "love." Here it means the lover's creative imagination.

15. **high fantastical:** capable of the highest flights of fancy.

41. for — —
and — — — —
his —

ACT I

Scene I. [The Duke's Palace.]

Enter Orsino (Duke of Illyria), Curio and other
Lords; [and Musicians].

Duke. If music be the food of love, play on;
Give me excess of it, that, surfeiting,
The appetite may sicken, and so die.
That strain again! It had a dying fall;
O, it came o'er my ear like the sweet sound   5
That breathes upon a bank of violets,
Stealing and giving odor! Enough, no more!
'Tis not so sweet now as it was before.
O spirit of love, how quick and fresh art thou,
That, notwithstanding thy capacity   10
Receiveth as the sea, naught enters there,
Of what validity and pitch soe'er,
But falls into abatement and low price
Even in a minute! So full of shapes is fancy
That it alone is high fantastical.   15
   Cur. Will you go hunt, my lord?
      Duke.   What, Curio?

I

18. **hart:** Curio means the male red deer, but the Duke indulges in a typical Elizabethan pun on "hart/heart."

22. **turned into a hart:** a reference to the story of Actaeon, who had the ill fortune while hunting to come upon the goddess Diana bathing in a pool and was changed by the wrathful goddess into a hart; his own hounds pursued him and tore him to pieces (Ovid, *Metamorphoses*, Book III).

23. **fell:** fierce, murderous.

28. **element:** heavens, sky; **till seven years' heat:** till the lapse of seven years.

30. **cloistress:** nun.

32-3. **season/ A brother's dead love:** preserve her love for a dead brother.

37. **the rich golden shaft:** Cupid's golden arrow, with which he induced love; a leaden-tipped arrow was used to provoke repulsion.

39. **liver:** the source of passionate love; **heart:** the originator of all emotions.

41. **Her sweet perfections:** i.e., liver, brain, and heart; **one self king:** one and one only man to rule her.

Cur. The hart.

Duke. Why, so I do, the noblest that I have.
O, when mine eyes did see Olivia first,   20
Methought she purged the air of pestilence!
That instant was I turned into a hart,
And my desires, like fell and cruel hounds,
E'er since pursue me.

Enter Valentine.

How now? What news from her?   25
Val. So please my lord, I might not be admitted.
But from her handmaid do return this answer:
The element itself, till seven years' heat,
Shall not behold her face at ample view;
But like a cloistress she will veiled walk,   30
And water once a day her chamber round
With eye-offending brine: all this to season
A brother's dead love, which she would keep fresh
And lasting in her sad remembrance.

Duke. O, she that hath a heart of that fine frame   35
To pay this debt of love but to a brother,
How will she love when the rich golden shaft
Hath killed the flock of all affections else
That live in her; when liver, brain, and heart,
These sovereign thrones, are all supplied and filled,   40
Her sweet perfections, with one self king!
Away before me to sweet beds of flowers!
Love-thoughts lie rich when canopied with bowers.
                      Exeunt.

I. ii. Viola has been cast ashore on the seacoast of Illyria. Her brother, Sebastian, has apparently been drowned. Viola decides to disguise herself as a man and seek service with Duke Orsino until the time seems appropriate to reveal herself.

4. Elysium: i.e., the Elysian Fields; Heaven.

13. driving: drifting.

15. practice: trick.

17. Arion on the dolphin's back: Arion was an ancient poet and musician, according to Herodotus, who jumped from the vessel taking him from Sicily to Corinth to escape the murderous intent of the sailors on board and was rescued by a dolphin.

18. hold acquaintance with: keep in company with; i.e., remain on the surface of the ocean.

21-3. Mine own escape unfoldeth to my hope,/ Whereto thy speech serves for authority,/ The like of him: my own escape reveals to my hope, and your words give me some justification, the possibility that he may have escaped in a similar way.

Scene II. [The seacoast.]

Enter Viola, *a* Captain, *and* Sailors.

Vio. What country, friends, is this?

Capt. This is Illyria, lady.

Vio. And what should I do in Illyria?
My brother he is in Elysium.
Perchance he is not drowned: what think you, sailors?   5

     Capt. It is perchance that you yourself were saved.

     Vio. O my poor brother! and so perchance may he
     be.

     Capt. True, madam; and, to comfort you with
     chance,   10
Assure yourself, after our ship did split,
When you, and those poor number saved with you,
Hung on our driving boat, I saw your brother,
Most provident in peril, bind himself
(Courage and hope both teaching him the practice)   15
To a strong mast that lived upon the sea;
Where, like Arion on the dolphin's back,
I saw him hold acquaintance with the waves
So long as I could see.

     Vio. For saying so, there's gold.   20
Mine own escape unfoldeth to my hope,
Whereto thy speech serves for authority,
The like of him. Knowst thou this country?

     Capt. Ay, madam, well, for I was bred and born
Not three hours' travel from this very place.   25

     Vio. Who governs here?

32. **late:** recently.

45-7. **delivered to the world,/ Till I had made mine own occasion mellow,/ What my estate is:** made known to the world as myself until I had arranged what seemed to me a ripe opportunity.

48. **were:** would be; **compass:** manage.

50. **not:** i.e., not even.

52. **though that:** though.

55. **thy fair and outward character:** what is handsomely written on your exterior; your fair appearance.

Actaeon.

From Andreas Alciati, *Emblemata* (1556).

(See I. i. 22.)

4

Capt. A noble duke, in nature as in name.

Vio. What is his name?

Capt. Orsino.

Vio. Orsino! I have heard my father name him.   30
He was a bachelor then.

Capt. And so is now, or was so very late;
For but a month ago I went from hence,
And then 'twas fresh in murmur (as you know
What great ones do, the less will prattle of)   35
That he did seek the love of fair Olivia.

Vio. What's she?

Capt. A virtuous maid, the daughter of a count
That died some twelvemonth since; then leaving her
In the protection of his son, her brother,   40
Who shortly also died; for whose dear love,
They say, she hath abjured the sight
And company of men.

Vio.   O that I served that lady,
And might not be delivered to the world,   45
Till I had made mine own occasion mellow,
What my estate is!

Capt.   That were hard to compass,
Because she will admit no kind of suit;
No, not the Duke's.   50

Vio. There is a fair behavior in thee, Captain;
And though that nature with a beauteous wall
Doth oft close in pollution, yet of thee
I will believe thou hast a mind that suits
With this thy fair and outward character.   55
I prithee (and I'll pay thee bounteously)
Conceal me what I am, and be my aid

58-9. haply shall become/ The form of my intent: may perhaps suit my intention.

60. eunuch: that is, a youth castrated in childhood to ensure the retention of a high tenor voice; such *castrati* were popular in Italy as singers.

63. allow me: cause me to be acknowledged.

65. shape thou thy silence to my wit: keep silent yourself about the disguise which my wit may fashion.

━━━━━━━━━━━━━━━━━━━━━━━

I. iii. Olivia's uncle, Sir Toby, complains to her waiting woman, Maria, of his niece's severity. Olivia tries, not too successfully, to curb Sir Toby's fondness for drunken reveling. Maria attempts to offer some good advice, but Sir Toby and his companion in frivolity, the foolish Sir Andrew Aguecheek, who has hopes of winning Olivia's hand, will not consent to give up their revelry.

━━━━━━━━━━━━━━

5. cousin: a term used of most near relatives.

7. except before excepted: a law term. Sir Toby is willing for his niece to object to his behavior as much as she likes—he intends to do as he pleases.

10. confine myself no finer than I am: dress no more finely than I am now dressed.

For such disguise as haply shall become
The form of my intent. I'll serve this duke.
Thou shalt present me as an eunuch to him;   60
It may be worth thy pains. For I can sing,
And speak to him in many sorts of music
That will allow me very worth his service.
What else may hap, to time I will commit;
Only shape thou thy silence to my wit.   65

Capt. Be you his eunuch, and your mute I'll be.
When my tongue blabs, then let mine eyes not see.

Vio. I thank thee. Lead me on.

Exeunt.

Scene III. [Olivia's house.]

Enter *Sir Toby* and *Maria.*

To. What a plague means my niece to take the
death of her brother thus? I am sure care's an enemy
to life.

Mar. By my troth, Sir Toby, you must come in
earlier o' nights. Your cousin, my lady, takes great   5
exceptions to your ill hours.

To. Why, let her except before excepted!

Mar. Ay, but you must confine yourself within the
modest limits of order.

To. Confine? I'll confine myself no finer than I am.   10
These clothes are good enough to drink in, and so be

12. **An:** if.

20. **tall:** brave.

21. **What's that to the purpose:** what's the relevance of that.

24. **very:** absolute.

25-6. **Fie:** in Elizabethan English fie was a stronger expletive than now, when it has become a sissy word; **viol de gamboys:** viol da gamba, a contemporary bass viol.

29. **natural:** i.e., like a natural (an idiot).

31. **gust:** gusto.

34-5. **substractors:** detractors, slanderers.

40. **coistrel:** a low-born, hence contemptible, fellow.

Arion.

From Andreas Alciati, *Emblemata* (1556).

(See I. ii. 17.)

these boots too. An they be not, let them hang themselves in their own straps.

Mar. That quaffing and drinking will undo you. I heard my lady talk of it yesterday; and of a foolish 15 knight that you brought in one night here to be her wooer.

To. Who? Sir Andrew Aguecheek?

Mar. Ay, he.

To. He's as tall a man as any's in Illyria. 20

Mar. What's that to the purpose?

To. Why, he has three thousand ducats a year.

Mar. Ay, but he'll have but a year in all these ducats. He's a very fool and a prodigal.

To. Fie that you'll say so! He plays o' the viol de 25 gamboys, and speaks three or four languages word for word without book, and hath all the good gifts of nature.

Mar. He hath, indeed, almost natural! for, besides that he's a fool, he's a great quarreler; and but that 30 he hath the gift of a coward to allay the gust he hath in quarreling, 'tis thought among the prudent he would quickly have the gift of a grave.

To. By this hand, they are scoundrels and substractors that say so of him. Who are they? 35

Mar. They that add, moreover, he's drunk nightly in your company.

To. With drinking healths to my niece. I'll drink to her as long as there is a passage in my throat and drink in Illyria. He's a coward and a coistrel that will 40 not drink to my niece till his brains turn o' the toe

42. a parish top: a large top frequently kept at the market place for the recreation of the local inhabitants; **Castiliano vulgo:** a garbled phrase, the meaning of which cannot be determined. Perhaps Sir Toby is merely using words that he hopes will impress Maria and influence her to restrain her contempt for Sir Andrew.

43. Agueface: a pun on Sir Andrew's last name, which meant "thin and pale-faced."

49. What's that: i.e., what's "accost."

60. let part so: allow the lady to take her leave without more compliment from you.

64. have fools in hand: are dealing with fools.

66. Marry: by the Virgin Mary, a mild oath.

69. buttery bar: i.e., drinking bar. Maria's meaning is drawn out of her by Aguecheek's questioning.

like a parish top. What, wench! Castiliano vulgo! for
here comes Sir Andrew Agueface.

Enter Sir Andrew.

And. Sir Toby Belch! How now, Sir Toby Belch?
To. Sweet Sir Andrew!　　　　　　　　　　　　45
And. Bless you, fair shrew.
Mar. And you too, sir.
To. Accost, Sir Andrew, accost.
And. What's that?
To. My niece's chambermaid.　　　　　　　　　50
And. Good Mistress Accost, I desire better ac-
quaintance.
Mar. My name is Mary, sir.
And. Good Mistress Mary Accost—
To. You mistake, knight. "Accost" is front her, 55
board her, woo her, assail her.
And. By my troth, I would not undertake her in
this company. Is that the meaning of "accost"?
Mar. Fare you well, gentlemen.
To. An thou let part so, Sir Andrew, would thou 60
mightst never draw sword again!
And. An you part so, mistress, I would I might
never draw sword again! Fair lady, do you think you
have fools in hand?
Mar. Sir, I have not you by the hand.　　　　　65
And. Marry, but you shall have! and here's my
hand.
Mar. Now, sir, thought is free. I pray you, bring
your hand to the buttery bar and let it drink.

70. **Wherefore:** why.

78. **barren:** without any further matter for jest, lacking contact with you.

79. **thou lackst a cup of canary:** you need a drink. **Canary** was a sweet wine from the Canary Islands.

83. **Christian or an ordinary man:** i.e., any other Christian (all equal in God's sight); the common run of mankind.

84-5. **beef . . . does harm to my wit:** a common contemporary belief.

93. **arts:** liberal arts.

96-7. **curl by:** Lewis Theobald's correction of the Folio's "coole my."

A drinking scene.
From a broadside ballad in the Roxburghe Collection.

And. Wherefore, sweetheart? What's your meta- 70
phor?

Mar. It's dry, sir.

And. Why, I think so. I am not such an ass but I
can keep my hand dry. But what's your jest?

Mar. A dry jest, sir. 75

And. Are you full of them?

Mar. Ay, sir, I have them at my fingers' ends.
Marry, now I let go your hand, I am barren.   *Exit.*

To. O knight, thou lackst a cup of canary! When
did I see thee so put down? 80

And. Never in your life, I think, unless you see
canary put me down. Methinks sometimes I have no
more wit than a Christian or an ordinary man has.
But I am a great eater of beef, and I believe that
does harm to my wit. 85

To. No question.

And. An I thought that, I'd forswear it. I'll ride
home tomorrow, Sir Toby.

To. Pourquoi, my dear knight?

And. What is *"pourquoi"*? Do, or not do? I would 90
I had bestowed that time in the tongues that I have
in fencing, dancing, and bear-baiting. O, had I but
followed the arts!

To. Then hadst thou had an excellent head of hair.

And. Why, would that have mended my hair? 95

To. Past question, for thou seest it will not curl
by nature.

And. But it becomes me well enough, does't not?

To. Excellent. It hangs like flax on a distaff; and I

102. **home:** go home. The omission of a verb in this way was a common grammatical construction.

104. **hard:** near.

108. **there's life in't:** that is, your suit has possibilities.

111. **altogether:** to the exclusion of everything else.

112. **kickshawses:** kickshaws, fanciful toys, from the French *quelque chose* (something).

113-14. **under the degree of my betters:** of no higher birth than myself.

115. **old:** experienced; that is, someone who has been dancing for years.

116. **galliard:** one of the lively dances of the period.

118. **mutton to't:** capers (condiments) were accompaniments for meat.

119. **back-trick:** a backward dance step.

122. **like:** likely.

123. **Mistress Mall's picture:** Mall was a common nickname for a woman; no specific person is meant.

125. **coranto:** another dance with quick steps.

126. **sink-a-pace:** cinquepace (five steps), a dance allied to the galliard.

hope to see a housewife take thee between her legs 100
and spin it off.

And. Faith, I'll home tomorrow, Sir Toby. Your
niece will not be seen; or if she be, it's four to one
she'll none of me. The Count himself here hard by
woos her.   105

To. She'll none o' the Count. She'll not match
above her degree, neither in estate, years, nor wit;
I have heard her swear't. Tut, there's life in't, man.

And. I'll stay a month longer. I am a fellow o'
the strangest mind i' the world. I delight in masques and 110
revels sometimes altogether.

To. Art thou good at these kickshawses, knight?

And. As any man in Illyria, whatsoever he be, under the degree of my betters; and yet I will not compare with an old man.   115

To. What is thy excellence in a galliard, knight?

And. Faith, I can cut a caper.

To. And I can cut the mutton to't.

And. And I think I have the back-trick simply as
strong as any man in Illyria.   120

To. Wherefore are these things hid? Wherefore
have these gifts a curtain before 'em? Are they like
to take dust, like Mistress Mall's picture? Why dost
thou not go to church in a galliard and come home
in a coranto? My very walk should be a jig. I would 125
not so much as make water but in a sink-a-pace.
What dost thou mean? Is it a world to hide virtues
in? I did think, by the excellent constitution of thy
leg, it was formed under the star of a galliard.

131. **stock:** stocking.

133. **Taurus:** the zodiacal sign of the bull, believed to govern **legs** and **thighs** according to some contemporary astrologers.

━━━━━━━━━━━━━━━━━━━━━━━━━━

I. iv. Viola, disguised as Cesario, has become a great favorite with Duke Orsino, who decides that he might be an effective messenger to send to Olivia. Cesario agrees but knows it will be a painful effort, for she has herself fallen in love with Orsino.

━━━━━━━━━━━━━━━━━━━

6. **call in question:** doubt.

11. **On your attendance:** at your service.

12. **aloof:** apart; detached from us. The Duke requests a private word with Cesario.

The sign of Taurus.
From Hyginus, *Fabularum liber* (1549).

10

And. Ay, 'tis strong, and it does indifferent well in 130
a flame-colored stock. Shall we set about some revels?

To. What shall we do else? Were we not born
under Taurus?

And. Taurus? That's sides and heart.

To. No, sir; it is legs and thighs. Let me see thee 135
caper. [*Sir Andrew dances.*] Ha, higher! Ha, ha, excellent!

Exeunt.

Scene IV. [The Duke's Palace.]

Enter *Valentine*, and *Viola* in man's attire.

Val. If the Duke continue these favors towards you,
Cesario, you are like to be much advanced. He hath
known you but three days, and already you are no
stranger.

Vio. You either fear his humor or my negligence, 5
that you call in question the continuance of his love.
Is he inconstant, sir, in his favors?

Val. No, believe me.

Enter *Duke*, *Curio*, and *Attendants*.

Vio. I thank you. Here comes the Count.

Duke. Who saw Cesario, ho? 10

Vio. On your attendance, my lord, here.

Duke. Stand you awhile aloof.—Cesario,

22. **leap all civil bounds:** overstep all bounds of courtesy.

26. **Surprise:** overcome, capture; **dear faith:** profound sincerity.

29. **nuncio's:** that is, **nuncio's** youth. **Nuncio** means messenger. In other words, an older, graver ambassador would not be as effective with Olivia.

33. **Diana:** the virgin goddess, the personification of virginity.

34. **rubious:** ruby-colored, red.

35. **sound:** that is, unflawed in its youthful purity.

36. **is semblative a woman's part:** resembles the characteristics of a woman.

37. **thy constellation is right apt:** the stars under which you were born, as evidenced by your characteristics, suit you particularly for this enterprise.

Thou knowst no less but all. I have unclasped
To thee the book even of my secret soul.
Therefore, good youth, address thy gait unto her;   15
Be not denied access, stand at her doors,
And tell them there thy fixed foot shall grow
Till thou have audience.

    Vio.   Sure, my noble lord,
If she be so abandoned to her sorrow   20
As it is spoke, she never will admit me.

    Duke. Be clamorous and leap all civil bounds
Rather than make unprofited return.

    Vio. Say I do speak with her, my lord, what then?

    Duke. O, then unfold the passion of my love;   25
Surprise her with discourse of my dear faith!
It shall become thee well to act my woes.
She will attend it better in thy youth
Than in a nuncio's of more grave aspect.

    Vio. I think not so, my lord.   30

    Duke.   Dear lad, believe it;
For they shall yet belie thy happy years
That say thou art a man. Diana's lip
Is not more smooth and rubious; thy small pipe
Is as the maiden's organ, shrill and sound,   35
And all is semblative a woman's part.
I know thy constellation is right apt
For this affair. Some four or five attend him—
All, if you will; for I myself am best
When least in company. Prosper well in this,   40
And thou shalt live as freely as thy lord
To call his fortunes thine.

44. barful strife: effort beset with difficulties.

━━━━━━━━━━━━━━━━━━━━━

I. v. Feste, the Clown of Olivia's household, makes a tardy reappearance and is warned by Maria that Olivia is likely to dismiss him. Feste, however, is confident that he can jest his way out of his difficulty. When Olivia appears, he gains her favor again despite the ill will of Malvolio, her steward, who does what he can to influence her against the Clown. The Duke's messenger is announced and Malvolio is sent to deny him entrance; but Viola-Cesario will accept no denial and Olivia finally admits him. Viola plays Cesario so well that Olivia is completely in love with the Duke's boy by the end of her interview and sends Malvolio after the youth with a ring and an invitation to return the next day.

━━━━━━━━━━━━━━━━━

Ent. Clown: the stage directions in the Folio always refer to this character as the Clown, though his name is given in dialogue as Feste.

6. fear no colors: proverbial: "Truth fears no colors [enemy flags]."

7. Make that good: prove that.

9. A good lenten answer: an answer good enough for Lent only; i.e., poor.

14-5. God give them wisdom that have it; and those that are fools, let them use their talents: May God help wise ones to make the best use of their knowledge; fools must get along as best they can with their feeble wits. Feste hopes to be able to jolly his mistress out of any anger she may feel at his absence.

20. bear it out: make it bearable.   12

Vio.   I'll do my best
To woo your lady. [*Aside*] Yet a barful strife!
Whoe'er I woo, myself would be his wife.   45

                           Exeunt.

Scene V. [Olivia's house.]

Enter *Maria* and *Clown*.

Mar. Nay, either tell me where thou hast been,
or I will not open my lips so wide as a bristle may
enter in way of thy excuse. My lady will hang thee
for thy absence.

Clown. Let her hang me! He that is well hanged   5
in this world needs to fear no colors.

Mar. Make that good.

Clown. He shall see none to fear.

Mar. A good lenten answer. I can tell thee where
that saying was born, of "I fear no colors."   10

Clown. Where, good Mistress Mary?

Mar. In the wars; and that may you be bold to say
in your foolery.

Clown. Well, God give them wisdom that have it;
and those that are fools, let them use their talents.   15

Mar. Yet you will be hanged for being so long ab-
sent; or to be turned away—is not that as good as a
hanging to you?

Clown. Many a good hanging prevents a bad marriage; and for turning away, let summer bear it out.   20

23. **points:** Maria's reply puns on another meaning of the word: laces which tied together the various parts of male attire.

25. **gaskins:** hose.

27-8. **If Sir Toby would leave drinking, thou wert as witty a piece of Eve's flesh as any in Illyria:** that is, if Toby could be distracted from his reveling, you would be as clever a wife as he could find.

32. **an't:** if it.

35. **Quinapalus:** a mythical sage whom Feste invents for the occasion.

41. **Go to:** be off. An exclamation used to express impatience, reproof, or simply to silence the speaker; **dry:** i.e., barren of invention.

42. **dishonest:** dishonorable, in that he has been slacking his duties and absenting himself without leave.

47. **botcher:** tailor who specialized in mending.

Mar. You are resolute then?

Clown. Not so, neither; but I am resolved on two
points.

Mar. That if one break, the other will hold; or if
both break, your gaskins fall.   25

Clown. Apt, in good faith; very apt. Well, go thy
way! If Sir Toby would leave drinking, thou wert as
witty a piece of Eve's flesh as any in Illyria.

Mar. Peace, you rogue; no more, o' that. Here
comes my lady. Make your excuse wisely, you were   30
best.   [*Exit.*]

Enter *Lady Olivia* with *Malvolio.*

Clown. Wit, an't be thy will, put me into good
fooling! Those wits that think they have thee do very
oft prove fools; and I that am sure I lack thee may
pass for a wise man. For what says Quinapalus?   35
"Better a witty fool than a foolish wit."—God bless
thee, lady!

Oli. Take the fool away.

Clown. Do you not hear, fellows? Take away the
lady.   40

Oli. Go to, y'are a dry fool! I'll no more of you. Besides, you grow dishonest.

Clown. Two faults, madonna, that drink and good
counsel will amend. For give the dry fool drink, then
is the fool not dry. Bid the dishonest man mend him-   45
self: if he mend, he is no longer dishonest; if he cannot, let the botcher mend him. Anything that's mended is but patched; virtue that transgresses is but

51-2. **so:** fine; all to the good; **there is no true cuckold but calamity:** since everyone is bound by Fortune as though wedded to her, when Fortune is untrue one is truly a cuckold (a wronged husband). The man afflicted with misfortune is personified as **calamity** in Feste's wise maxim.

56. **Misprision:** misunderstanding, error.

57. **cucullus non facit monachum:** proverbial: A cowl does not make a monk—and by the same token, Feste indicates, my fool's uniform does not make me a fool in earnest.

58. **motley:** the particolored garb of professional fools.

61. **Dexteriously:** a variant form of "dexterously."

63-4. **Good my mouse of virtue:** my good little virtuous mouse. Feste relies on a fool's license in speaking so familiarly to his mistress. The position of **Good** is common Elizabethan grammatical usage.

65. **idleness:** that is, idle pastime; **bide:** await; that is, hear you out.

75. **mend:** improve.

77-8. **Infirmity . . . doth ever make the better fool:** that is, the more age weakens his intellect, the more foolish a man becomes.

14

patched with sin, and sin that amends is but patched
with virtue. If that this simple syllogism will serve, 50
so; if it will not, what remedy? As there is no true
cuckold but calamity, so beauty's a flower. The lady
bade take away the fool; therefore, I say again, take
her away.

Oli. Sir, I bade them take away you. 55

Clown. Misprision in the highest degree! Lady,
cucullus non facit monachum. That's as much to say
as, I wear not motley in my brain. Good madonna,
give me leave to prove you a fool.

Oli. Can you do it? 60

Clown. Dexteriously, good madonna.

Oli. Make your proof.

Clown. I must catechize you for it, madonna. Good
my mouse of virtue, answer me.

Oli. Well, sir, for want of other idleness, I'll bide 65
your proof.

Clown. Good madonna, why mournest thou?

Oli. Good fool, for my brother's death.

Clown. I think his soul is in hell, madonna.

Oli. I know his soul is in heaven, fool. 70

Clown. The more fool, madonna, to mourn for
your brother's soul being in heaven. Take away the
fool, gentlemen.

Oli. What think you of this fool, Malvolio? Doth
he not mend? 75

Mal. Yes, and shall do till the pangs of death shake
him. Infirmity, that decays the wise, doth ever make
the better fool.

Clown. God send you, sir, a speedy infirmity, for

85. **barren:** witless.

85-6. **put down . . . with:** defeated by; **an ordinary fool:** a common fool, such as were sometimes hired to entertain guests in a tavern.

87. **out of his guard:** a term from fencing: no longer able to defend himself; at a loss for a reply.

88. **minister occasion:** give opportunity.

90. **these set kind of fools:** i.e., fools with so little talent for improvisation, who are lost if their prepared line of humor goes unappreciated.

91. **zanies:** minor clowns.

92. **sick of self-love:** that is, vanity is your ailment.

93. **distempered:** disordered.

95-8. **bird bolts:** arrows with blunt tips used in hunting small birds for the pot—comparatively harmless missiles; **deem:** judge; **There is no slander in an allowed fool, though he do nothing but rail; nor no railing in a known discreet man, though he do nothing but reprove:** just as a licensed fool can get away with slander, so a man of noted discretion is forgiven his censure of others for the sake of his wisdom.

99-100. **Now Mercury indue thee with leasing, for thou speakest well of fools:** Mercury (the god noted for his trickiness) endow thee with the art of lying—you will need such aid if you will speak well of fools.

the better increasing your folly! Sir Toby will be 80
sworn that I am no fox; but he will not pass his word
for twopence that you are no fool.

Oli. How say you to that, Malvolio?

Mal. I marvel your ladyship takes delight in such
a barren rascal. I saw him put down the other day 85
with an ordinary fool that has no more brain than a
stone. Look you now, he's out of his guard already.
Unless you laugh and minister occasion to him, he is
gagged. I protest I take these wise men that crow so
at these set kind of fools no better than the fools' 90
zanies.

Oli. O, you are sick of self-love, Malvolio, and taste
with a distempered appetite. To be generous, guilt-
less, and of free disposition, is to take those things
for bird bolts that you deem cannon bullets. There 95
is no slander in an allowed fool, though he do nothing but rail; nor no railing in a known discreet man,
though he do nothing but reprove.

Clown. Now Mercury indue thee with leasing, for
thou speakest well of fools! 100

Enter *Maria*.

Mar. Madam, there is at the gate a young gentleman much desires to speak with you.

Oli. From the Count Orsino, is it?

Mar. I know not, madam. 'Tis a fair young man,
and well attended. 105

Oli. Who of my people hold him in delay?

Mar. Sir Toby, madam, your kinsman.

112. **old:** stale.

118. **pia mater:** brain.

123-24. **A plague o' these pickle-herring:** with drunken cunning, Sir Toby sidesteps the accusation that a hiccup was induced by drink; **sot:** blockhead, fool.

132. **give me faith:** that is, faith to combat the devil.

Oli. Fetch him off, I pray you. He speaks nothing
but madman. Fie on him! [*Exit Maria.*] Go you,
Malvolio. If it be a suit from the Count, I am sick, or   110
not at home. What you will, to dismiss it. (*Exit Malvolio.*) Now you see, sir, how your fooling grows old,
and people dislike it.

Clown. Thou hast spoke for us, madonna, as if thy
eldest son should be a fool; whose skull Jove cram   115
with brains!

Enter Sir Toby.

for—here he comes—one of thy kin has a most weak
pia mater.

Oli. By mine honor, half drunk! What is he at the
gate, cousin?   120

To. A gentleman.

Oli. A gentleman? What gentleman?

To. 'Tis a gentleman here. A plague o' these pickle-
herring! How now, sot?

Clown. Good Sir Toby!   125

Oli. Cousin, cousin, how have you come so early
by this lethargy?

To. Lechery? I defy lechery. There's one at the
gate.

Oli. Ay, marry, what is he?   130

To. Let him be the Devil an he will, I care not!
Give me faith, say I. Well, it's all one.   *Exit.*

Oli. What's a drunken man like, fool?

Clown. Like a drowned man, a fool, and a mad-

135. **heat:** enough to warm him through.

137-38. **crowner:** coroner; **sit o':** hold an inquest on the case of.

143-44. **takes on him to understand so much:** pretends to know as much.

150. **Has:** he has.

151. **a sheriff's post:** in Elizabethan England it was customary to set up a post by the house of the local sheriff.

160. **squash:** unripe peasecod (pea pod).

161. **codling:** green apple.

162. **in standing water:** i.e., halfway, like a tide between ebb and flow.

192. **from my commission:** irrelevant to my embassy.
195. **forgive:** excuse the omission of.
199. **feigned:** insincere.
203-4. **'Tis not that time of moon with me to make one in so skipping a dialogue:** that is, it is the wrong quarter of the moon to influence me; I am not at the moment lunatic enough for frivolous conversation of this type.
206. **swabber:** clearer of the decks; **hull:** lie becalmed.
207. **giant:** a facetious term for Maria, who is elsewhere described in terms that make it clear she is unusually small.
213. **taxation:** demand.

man. One draught above heat makes him a fool, the 135 second mads him, and a third drowns him.

Oli. Go thou and seek the crowner, and let him sit o' my coz; for he's in the third degree of drink—he's drowned. Go look after him.

Clown. He is but mad yet, madonna, and the fool 140 shall look to the madman.   [*Exit.*]

Enter *Malvolio*.

Mal. Madam, yond young fellow swears he will speak with you. I told him you were sick: he takes on him to understand so much, and therefore comes to speak with you. I told him you were asleep: he 145 seems to have a foreknowledge of that too, and therefore comes to speak with you. What is to be said to him, lady? He's fortified against any denial.

Oli. Tell him he shall not speak with me.

Mal. Has been told so; and he says he'll stand at 150 your door like a sheriff's post, and be the supporter to a bench, but he'll speak with you.

Oli. What kind o' man is he?

Mal. Why, of mankind.

Oli. What manner of man?   155

Mal. Of very ill manner. He'll speak with you, will you or no.

Oli. Of what personage and years is he?

Mal. Not yet old enough for a man nor young enough for a boy; as a squash is before 'tis a peasecod, 160 or a codling when 'tis almost an apple. 'Tis with him in standing water, between boy and man. He is very

163. **well-favored:** handsome; **shrewishly:** in a shrill voice.

177. **con:** learn.

178-79. **comptible, even to the least sinister usage:** that is, she takes personal account of the smallest discourtesy and is affected by it.

183. **modest:** reasonable.

185. **comedian:** actor.

186. **my profound heart:** a further elaborate compliment to Olivia.

DONNA NOBILE INGLESE.

A highborn Englishwoman.
From Cesare Vecellio, *De gli habiti antichi et moderni* (1590).

18

well-favored and he speaks very shrewish would think his mother's milk were scarce him.

Oli. Let him approach. Call in my gentlew
Mal. Gentlewoman, my lady calls.

Enter *Maria*.

Oli. Give me my veil; come, throw it o'er We'll once more hear Orsino's embassy.

Enter *Viola*.

Vio. The honorable lady of the house, she?

Oli. Speak to me; I shall answer for her.

Vio. Most radiant, exquisite, and unn beauty—I pray you tell me if this be the la house, for I never saw her. I would be loa away my speech; for, besides that it is e well penned, I have taken great pains to co beauties, let me sustain no scorn. I am ver ble, even to the least sinister usage.

Oli. Whence came you, sir?

Vio. I can say little more than I have st that question's out of my part. Good gentle me modest assurance if you be the lady of that I may proceed in my speech.

Oli. Are you a comedian?

Vio. No, my profound heart; and yet (h

fangs of malice I swear) I am not that I play. Are
you the lady of the house?

Oli. If I do not usurp myself, I am.

Vio. Most certain, if you are she, you do usurp 190
yourself; for what is yours to bestow is not yours to
reserve. But this is from my commission. I will on
with my speech in your praise and then show you
the heart of my message.

Oli. Come to what is important in't. I forgive you 195
the praise. ·

Vio. Alas, I took great pains to study it, and 'tis
poetical.

Oli. It is the more like to be feigned; I pray you
keep it in. I heard you were saucy at my gates; and 200
allowed your approach rather to wonder at you than
to hear you. If you be not mad, be gone; if you have
reason, be brief. 'Tis not that time of moon with me
to make one in so skipping a dialogue.

Mar. Will you hoist sail, sir? Here lies your way. 205

Vio. No, good swabber; I am to hull here a little
longer. Some mollification for your giant, sweet lady!

Oli. Tell me your mind.

Vio. I am a messenger.

Oli. Sure you have some hideous matter to deliver, 210
when the courtesy of it is so fearful. Speak your office.

Vio. It alone concerns your ear. I bring no overture
of war, no taxation of homage. I hold the olive in
my hand. My words are as full of peace as matter.

Oli. Yet you began rudely. What are you? What 215
would you?

Vio. The rudeness that hath appeared in me have

218. **entertainment:** reception.

220. **divinity:** sacred conversation.

228. **by the method:** i.e., in the manner of a preacher giving a sermon, in accordance with Olivia's questions.

234-35. **out of your text:** that is, having moved from hearts to faces.

236-37. **such a one I was this present:** Olivia continues to speak as though her face is a painted portrait: her unveiled face is a lifelike portrait of her beauty at the present moment.

239. **in grain:** a phrase meaning "permanently dyed." **Grain** was a dye obtained from cochineal.

248-49. **labeled to my will:** set forth on a sheet attached to my will.

I learned from my entertainment. What I am, and what I would, are as secret as maidenhead: to your ears, divinity; to any other's, profanation.   220

Oli. Give us the place alone; we will hear this divinity. [*Exit Maria.*] Now, sir, what is your text?

Vio. Most sweet lady—

Oli. A comfortable doctrine, and much may be said of it. Where lies your text?   225

Vio. In Orsino's bosom.

Oli. In his bosom? In what chapter of his bosom?

Vio. To answer by the method, in the first of his heart.

Oli. O, I have read it! it is heresy. Have you no more to say?   230

Vio. Good madam, let me see your face.

Oli. Have you any commission from your lord to negotiate with my face? You are now out of your text. But we will draw the curtain and show you the picture. [*Unveils.*] Look you, sir, such a one I was this present. Is't not well done?   235

Vio. Excellently done, if God did all.

Oli. 'Tis in grain, sir; 'twill endure wind and weather.   240

Vio. 'Tis beauty truly blent, whose red and white Nature's own sweet and cunning hand laid on.
Lady, you are the cruel'st she alive
If you will lead these graces to the grave,
And leave the world no copy.   245

Oli. O, sir, I will not be so hard-hearted. I will give out divers schedules of my beauty. It shall be inventoried, and every particle and utensil labeled to

251. **praise:** probably a pun on "praise/appraise."

258. **fertile:** plentiful.

264. **In voices well divulged:** according to general report; **free:** liberal, generous.

265. **in dimension and the shape of nature:** i.e., in the physique that nature has given him.

266. **gracious:** graced with physical beauty.

268. **in my master's flame:** with the same flaming ardor my master feels.

269. **such a suff'ring, such a deadly life:** i.e., suffering so much for lack of your love that life is like a lingering death.

274. **my soul within the house:** that is, his mistress—Olivia.

275. **cantons of contemned love:** songs lamenting my despised love.

277. **reverberate:** reverberating, echoing.

278. **the babbling gossip of the air:** Echo.

my will:—as, item, two lips, indifferent red; item, two
grey eyes, with lids to them; item, one neck, one 250
chin, and so forth. Were you sent hither to praise me?

Vio. I see you what you are—you are too proud;
But if you were the Devil, you are fair.
My lord and master loves you. O, such love
Could be but recompensed though you were crowned 255
The nonpareil of beauty!

Oli.   How does he love me?

Vio. With adorations, fertile tears,
With groans that thunder love, with sighs of fire.

Oli. Your lord does know my mind; I cannot love 260
    him.
Yet I suppose him virtuous, know him noble,
Of great estate, of fresh and stainless youth;
In voices well divulged, free, learned, and valiant,
And in dimension and the shape of nature 265
A gracious person. But yet I cannot love him.
He might have took his answer long ago.

Vio. If I did love you in my master's flame,
With such a suff'ring, such a deadly life,
In your denial I would find no sense; 270
I would not understand it.

Oli.   Why, what would you?

Vio. Make me a willow cabin at your gate
And call upon my soul within the house;
Write loyal cantons of contemned love 275
And sing them loud even in the dead of night;
Halloa your name to the reverberate hills
And make the babbling gossip of the air
Cry out "Olivia!" O, you should not rest

281. **But you should pity me:** unless you took pity upon me.

290. **fee'd post:** paid messenger.

292. **make his heart of flint that you shall love:** i.e., make the man you come to love flint-hearted.

299. **give thee fivefold blazon:** proclaim you five times over. A **blazon** was a description in heraldic terms, or a heraldic shield; **soft:** slowly, just a minute.

Between the elements of air and earth   280
But you should pity me!

    Oli. You might do much. What is your parentage?

    Vio. Above my fortunes, yet my state is well.
I am a gentleman.

    Oli.   Get you to your lord.   285
I cannot love him. Let him send no more,
Unless, perchance, you come to me again
To tell me how he takes it. Fare you well.
I thank you for your pains. Spend this for me.

    Vio. I am no fee'd post, lady; keep your purse;   290
My master, not myself, lacks recompense.
Love make his heart of flint that you shall love;
And let your fervor, like my master's, be
Placed in contempt! Farewell, fair cruelty.   *Exit.*

    Oli. "What is your parentage?"   295
"Above my fortunes, yet my state is well.
I am a gentleman." I'll be sworn thou art.
Thy tongue, thy face, thy limbs, actions, and spirit
Do give thee fivefold blazon. Not too fast! soft, soft!
Unless the master were the man. How now?   300
Even so quickly may one catch the plague?
Methinks I feel this youth's perfections
With an invisible and subtle stealth
To creep in at mine eyes. Well, let it be.
What ho, Malvolio!   305

             Enter *Malvolio.*

    Mal.   Here, madam, at your service.

    Oli. Run after that same peevish messenger,

308. County: Count.

313. Hie: hurry.

315-16. fear to find/ Mine eye too great a flatterer for my mind: fear that I will discover in time that my eye has beguiled me into a passion for one whom my judgment would reject.

317. Ourselves we do not owe: we do not own ourselves; we have no control over our fates.

GIOVANE
INGLESE

An English youth.
From Cesare Vecellio, *De gli habiti antichi et moderni* (1590).

23

The County's man. He left this ring behind him,
Would I or not. Tell him I'll none of it.
Desire him not to flatter with his lord   310
Nor hold him up with hopes. I am not for him.
If that the youth will come this way tomorrow,
I'll give him reasons for't. Hie thee, Malvolio.

   Mal. Madam, I will.   *Exit.*

   Oli. I do I know not what, and fear to find   315
Mine eye too great a flatterer for my mind.
Fate, show thy force! Ourselves we do not owe.
What is decreed must be—and be this so!

                              [Exit.]

TWELFTH NIGHT

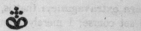

ACT II

II. i. Sebastian and his rescuer, Antonio, have also come ashore on the seacoast of Illyria. Sebastian does not know his sister's fate and assumes that she is drowned. When he decides to set out for Orsino's court, Antonio, because of his great affection for Sebastian, determines to follow, though he knows that he has been outlawed in Orsino's realm.

<hr>

3. **By your patience:** by your allowance; if you will excuse me.

10-1. **sooth:** truly; **My determinate voyage is mere extravagancy:** that is, I have determined on no set course; I merely plan to wander. "Extravagant" was often used to mean "wandering."

14. **in manners:** as a matter of courtesy.

18-9. **in an hour:** in the same hour: i.e., twins.

ACT II

Scene I. [The seacoast.]

Enter *Antonio* and *Sebastian.*

Ant. Will you stay no longer? nor will you not that
I go with you?

Seb. By your patience, no. My stars shine darkly
over me; the malignancy of my fate might perhaps
distemper yours. Therefore I shall crave of you your   5
leave, that I may bear my evils alone. It were a bad
recompense for your love to lay any of them on you.

Ant. Let me yet know of you whither you are
bound.

Seb. No, sooth, sir. My determinate voyage is mere   10
extravagancy. But I perceive in you so excellent a
touch of modesty that you will not extort from me
what I am willing to keep in; therefore it charges me
in manners the rather to express myself. You must
know of me then, Antonio, my name is Sebastian,   15
which I called Roderigo. My father was that Sebastian of Messaline whom I know you have heard of.
He left behind him myself and a sister, both born in
an hour. If the heavens had been pleased, would we
had so ended! But you, sir, altered that, for some hour   20

24

21. **breach:** breaking waves.

26. **with such estimable wonder:** despite my esteem and admiration for her.

28. **envy:** that is, even a malicious judge.

31. **more:** i.e., his salt tears.

32. **bad entertainment:** i.e., less than cordial reception on these shores; see **entertainment,** I. v. 218.

34. **murder me:** that is, by depriving me of your company; **for:** in exchange for.

39. **the manners of my mother:** womanlike behavior in crying.

before you took me from the breach of the sea was
my sister drowned.

Ant. Alas the day!

Seb. A lady, sir, though it was said she much re-
sembled me, was yet of many accounted beautiful. 25
But though I could not with such estimable wonder
overfar believe that, yet thus far I will boldly publish
her: she bore a mind that envy could not but call
fair. She is drowned already, sir, with salt water,
though I seem to drown her remembrance again with 30
more.

Ant. Pardon me, sir, your bad entertainment.

Seb. O good Antonio, forgive me your trouble!

Ant. If you will not murder me for my love, let me
be your servant. 35

Seb. If you will not undo what you have done, that
is, kill him whom you have recovered, desire it not.
Fare ye well at once. My bosom is full of kindness;
and I am yet so near the manners of my mother that,
upon the least occasion more, mine eyes will tell tales 40
of me. I am bound to the Count Orsino's court. Farewell.
                                   Exit.

Ant. The gentleness of all the gods go with thee!
I have many enemies in Orsino's court,
Else would I very shortly see thee there. 45
But come what may, I do adore thee so
That danger shall seem sport, and I will go.
                                     Exit.

II. ii. Malvolio overtakes Cesario and "returns" the ring which Olivia has said he left. Cesario is puzzled and fearful that Olivia has been smitten by her masculine disguise, since she left no ring from Orsino.

Ent. at several doors: i.e., they have been going their separate ways and meet on stage.

1. **even:** just; see I. i. 14.
8. **desperate:** without hope.
20. **her eyes had lost her tongue:** her close scrutiny of me had robbed her of the ability to speak.

Scene II. [A street.]

Enter Viola *and* Malvolio *at several doors.*

Mal. Were not you even now with the Countess Olivia?

Vio. Even now, sir. On a moderate pace I have since arrived but hither.

Mal. She returns this ring to you, sir. You might 5
have saved me my pains, to have taken it away your-self. She adds, moreover, that you should put your lord into a desperate assurance she will none of him. And one thing more, that you be never so hardy to come again in his affairs, unless it be to report your 10
lord's taking of this. Receive it so.

Vio. She took the ring of me. I'll none of it.

Mal. Come, sir, you peevishly threw it to her; and her will is, it should be so returned. If it be worth stooping for, there it lies, in your eye; if not, be it 15
his that finds it.   *Exit.*

Vio. I left no ring with her. What means this lady?
Fortune forbid my outside have not charmed her!
She made good view of me; indeed, so much
That methought her eyes had lost her tongue,   20
For she did speak in starts distractedly.
She loves me sure; the cunning of her passion
Invites me in this churlish messenger.
None of my lord's ring? Why, he sent her none!
I am the man. If it be so—as 'tis—   25
Poor lady, she were better love a dream!

28. **the pregnant enemy:** i.e., the Devil, who is ever alert to opportunity.

29. **the proper false:** a handsome man who is not what he seems.

32. **such as we are made of, such we be:** being made of fragile stuff, we can only behave like the frail creatures we are.

33. **How will this fadge:** how will all this work out. Fadge means succeed.

34. **monster:** neither man nor woman at present; **fond:** a verb: dote.

39. **thriftless:** profitless; without hope of success.

▬▬▬▬▬▬▬▬▬▬▬▬▬▬

II. iii. Sir Toby and Sir Andrew, Feste, and Maria are reveling late and making so much noise that Malvolio is aroused to interfere. Failing to dampen their high spirits, he goes off to tell Olivia; the revelers, led by Maria, decide to get even with him. Maria proposes to trick him with a love letter which he will think Olivia has written.

▬▬▬▬▬▬▬

2. **is to be up betimes:** i.e., is the same as getting up early; **diluculo surgere:** the beginning of a quotation from Lily's Latin Grammar: *"Diluculo surgere saluberrimum est"*: "To rise early is most healthful." This is an early form of the proverb that Benjamin Franklin popularized as "Early to bed and early to rise, etc."

Disguise, I see thou art a wickedness
Wherein the pregnant enemy does much.
How easy is it for the proper false
In women's waxen hearts to set their forms!   30
Alas, our frailty is the cause, not we!
For such as we are made of, such we be.
How will this fadge? My master loves her dearly;
And I (poor monster) fond as much on him;
And she (mistaken) seems to dote on me.   35
What will become of this? As I am man,
My state is desperate for my master's love.
As I am woman (now alas the day!),
What thriftless sighs shall poor Olivia breathe!
O Time, thou must untangle this, not I;   40
It is too hard a knot for me t'untie!

                                        [*Exit.*]

Scene III. [Olivia's house.]

Enter *Sir Toby* and *Sir Andrew.*

To. Approach, Sir Andrew. Not to be abed after
midnight is to be up betimes; and "*diluculo surgere*,"
thou knowst—

And. Nay, by my troth, I know not; but I know to
be up late is to be up late.   5

To. A false conclusion! I hate it as an unfilled can.
To be up after midnight, and to go to bed then, is

9-10. our life: i.e., human life; **the four elements:** fire, air, earth, and water, which were believed to make up the human body.

12. eating and drinking: Sir Andrew, with great practicality, points out that life would cease without these functions, regardless of the four elements.

14. stoup: tankard.

16. hearts: hearties.

17. the picture of We Three: the reference is to a satirical picture, used as an inn sign more than once, of two obvious idiots or fools with the legend "We Three," or more explicitly, "We three loggerheads be"; the observer is the third.

18. catch: a type of song also known as a round.

19. breast: voice.

23-4. Pigrogromitus, of the Vapians passing the equinoctial of Queubus: Sir Andrew is attempting to recall meaningless words used by the Clown to impress him.

25. leman: lady love.

26. impeticos thy gratillity: impetticoat your little gratuity; that is, gave it to my sweetheart. The Clown again uses nonsensical words for Sir Andrew's benefit and though Sir Andrew does not understand a word he says, he pretends to be vastly amused.

28. Myrmidons: the troops of Achilles, but the rest of the Clown's speech is pure foolery.

33-4. testril: a coined word probably meaning "little sixpence," from the French, *teston;* **give a:** the Folio has no terminating punctuation and the rest of the line may have been omitted in printing. Sir Andrew's thought can probably be completed with the words "another should do likewise."

early; so that to go to bed after midnight is to go to
bed betimes. Does not our life consist of the four elements?   10

And. Faith, so they say; but I think it rather con-
sists of eating and drinking.

To. Th'art a scholar! Let us therefore eat and
drink. Marian I say! a stoup of wine!

Enter *Clown.*

And. Here comes the fool, i' faith.   15

Clown. How now, my hearts? Did you never see
the picture of We Three?

To. Welcome, ass. Now let's have a catch.

And. By my troth, the fool has an excellent breast.
I had rather than forty shillings I had such a leg, and   20
so sweet a breath to sing, as the fool has. In sooth,
thou wast in very gracious fooling last night, when
thou spokest of Pigrogromitus, of the Vapians passing
the equinoctial of Queubus. 'Twas very good, i' faith.
I sent thee sixpence for thy leman. Hadst it?   25

Clown. I did impeticos thy gratillity; for Malvolio's
nose is no whipstock. My lady has a white hand, and
the Myrmidons are no bottle-ale houses.

And. Excellent! Why, this is the best fooling,
when all is done. Now a song!   30

To. Come on! there is sixpence for you. Let's have
a song.

And. There's a testril of me too. If one knight give
a—

35-6. of good life: i.e., with a moral.

51. sweet and twenty: various interpretations have been suggested; one that the phrase refers to the age of the beauty; another that it means give me a score of sweet kisses; and a third that it means sweet in the twentieth degree.

54. contagious breath: a catchy voice, with a pun.

56. To hear by the nose, it is dulcet in contagion: in apprehending his voice by our noses, we get a sweet sound but a contagious scent.

Clown. Would you have a love song, or a song of   35
good life?

To. A love song, a love song.

And. Ay, ay! I care not for good life.

Clown sings.

O mistress mine, where are you roaming?
O, stay and hear! your truelove's coming,   40
    That can sing both high and low.
Trip no further, pretty sweeting;
Journeys end in lovers meeting,
    Every wise man's son doth know.

And. Excellent good, i' faith!   45
To. Good, good!

Clown [sings].

What is love? 'Tis not hereafter;
Present mirth hath present laughter;
    What's to come is still unsure:
In delay there lies no plenty;   50
Then come kiss me, sweet and twenty!
    Youth's a stuff will not endure.

And. A mellifluous voice, as I am true knight.
To. A contagious breath.
And. Very sweet and contagious, i' faith.   55
To. To hear by the nose, it is dulcet in contagion.

57. **welkin:** sky, heavens.

58-9. **draw three souls out of one weaver:** i.e., so charm the ear as to draw forth not only the weaver's soul but two additional souls. In Shakespeare's time, many weavers were Puritans, given to piety and psalm-singing. This may be a gibe at the precise sect.

60. **dog:** expert.

64. **Thou knave:** a catch in which each of the singers in turn is called "Thou knave" by the others.

67. **'Tis not the first time:** Sir Andrew boasts that he is a formidable fellow who has often taunted another to the point of being called a knave—the prelude to a fight.

75. **Cataian:** the name for a native of China (Cathay). The Chinese had a reputation for sharp dealing and the word is usually used in contemporary works to indicate general untrustworthiness or contempt. Sir Toby merely dismisses Olivia; drink has made him careless of consequences; **politicians:** shrewd fellows.

76-7. **Peg-a-Ramsey:** Sir Toby means to apply some vague derogatory epithet to Malvolio but in his drunken state his meaning is not clearly expressed. **Peg-a-Ramsey** was the name of a merry song and dance tune; **Three merry men be we:** another old song; **consanguineous:** related to Olivia by blood, as Sir Toby goes on to make clear.

78. **Tilly-vally:** meaningless phrase, cf. "fiddle-faddle" and similar nonsense interjections.

80. **Beshrew:** curse; used as a light oath.

But shall we make the welkin dance indeed? Shall
we rouse the night owl in a catch that will draw three
souls out of one weaver? Shall we do that?

And. An you love me, let's do't! I am dog at a   60
catch.

Clown. By'r Lady, sir, and some dogs will catch
well.

And. Most certain. Let our catch be "Thou knave."

Clown. "Hold thy peace, thou knave," knight? I   65
shall be constrained in't to call thee knave, knight.

And. 'Tis not the first time I have constrained one
to call me knave. Begin, fool. It begins, "Hold thy
peace."

Clown. I shall never begin if I hold my peace.   70

And. Good, i' faith! Come, begin.

Catch sung. Enter *Maria.*

Mar. What a caterwauling do you keep here! If
my lady have not called up her steward Malvolio and
bid him turn you out of doors, never trust me.

To. My lady's a Cataian, we are politicians, Mal-   75
volio's a Peg-a-Ramsey, and [*Sings*] "Three merry
men be we." Am not I consanguineous? Am I not of
her blood? Tilly-vally, lady! [*Sings*] "There dwelt a
man in Babylon, lady, lady!"

Clown. Beshrew me, the knight's in admirable   80
fooling.

And. Ay, he does well enough if he be disposed,
and so do I too. He does it with a better grace, but
I do it more natural.

88. honesty: regard for honor, decency.

91. coziers: cobblers.

94-5. Sneck up: be hanged.

96. round: blunt.

98. she's nothing allied to your disorders: she will have no part of your disorderly actions.

103-4. Farewell . . . gone: these lines and the excerpts that follow are all from the same song, "Corydon's Farewell to Phyllis."

A merry tinker.
From a broadside ballad in the Roxburghe Collection.

To. [*Sings*] "O' the twelfth day of December"—   85
Mar. For the love o' God, peace!

Enter *Malvolio.*

Mal. My masters, are you mad? or what are you?
Have you no wit, manners, nor honesty, but to gab-
ble like tinkers at this time of night? Do ye make an
alehouse of my lady's house, that ye squeak out your   90
coziers' catches without any mitigation or remorse of
voice? Is there no respect of place, persons, nor time
in you?

To. We did keep time, sir, in our catches. Sneck
up!   95

Mal. Sir Toby, I must be round with you. My lady
bade me tell you that, though she harbors you as her
kinsman, she's nothing allied to your disorders. If you
can separate yourself and your misdemeanors, you
are welcome to the house. If not, and it would please   100
you to take leave of her, she is very willing to bid
you farewell.

To. [*Sings*] "Farewell, dear heart, since I must
    needs be gone."

Mar. Nay, good Sir Toby!   105

Clown. [*Sings*] "His eyes do show his days are
    almost done."

Mal. Is't even so?

To. "But I will never die."

Clown. Sir Toby, there you lie.   110

Mal. This is much credit to you!

119. **ginger:** used to spice ale.

121-22. **rub your chain with crumbs:** i.e., polish up your chain (the badge of his position as steward).

125. **uncivil rule:** disorderly behavior.

127. **Go shake your ears:** i.e., like an ass.

128-30. **'Twere as good a deed as to drink when a man's ahungry, to challenge him the field, and then to break promise with him and make a fool of him:** Sir Andrew fuzzily contemplates treating Malvolio in this uncivil fashion.

135-36. **let me alone with him:** i.e., let me handle him; **gull:** dupe, fool.

140. **Possess:** inform.

To. "Shall I bid him go?"

Clown. "What an if you do?"

To. "Shall I bid him go, and spare not?"

Clown. "O, no, no, no, no, you dare not!"　115

To. Out o' tune, sir? Ye lie. Art any more than a steward? Dost thou think, because thou art virtuous, there shall be no more cakes and ale?

Clown. Yes, by Saint Anne! and ginger shall be hot i' the mouth too.　120

To. Th'art i' the right.—Go, sir, rub your chain with crumbs. A stoup of wine, Maria!

Mal. Mistress Mary, if you prized my lady's favor at anything more than contempt, you would not give means for this uncivil rule. She shall know of it, by this hand.　125　　　　　　　　　　　　　　　　*Exit.*

Mar. Go shake your ears!

And. 'Twere as good a deed as to drink when a man's ahungry, to challenge him the field, and then to break promise with him and make a fool of him.　130

To. Do't, knight. I'll write thee a challenge; or I'll deliver thy indignation to him by word of mouth.

Mar. Sweet Sir Toby, be patient for tonight. Since the youth of the Count's was today with my lady, she is much out of quiet. For Monsieur Malvolio, let　135 me alone with him. If I do not gull him into a nayword, and make him a common recreation, do not think I have wit enough to lie straight in my bed. I know I can do it.

To. Possess us, possess us! Tell us something of him.　140

Mar. Marry, sir, sometimes he is a kind of Puritan.

148. constantly: invariably; **a time-pleaser:** one who follows the prevailing wind; **affectioned:** affected.

149-50. cons state without book: learns stately deportment by heart; **utters it by great swarths:** distributes it largely. **Swarth** is a variant form of "swath"; **the best persuaded of himself:** holding the best opinion of himself.

160. feelingly personated: convincingly characterized.

161. on a forgotten matter: in instances where we no longer remember the circumstances concerning a piece of writing.

Penthesilea.

From Guillaume Rouille, *Del prontuario de le medaglie de piu illustri, & fulgenti huomini & donne* (1553).

(See II. iii. 177.)

And. O, if I thought that, I'd beat him like a dog!

To. What, for being a Puritan? Thy exquisite reason, dear knight?

And. I have no exquisite reason for't, but I have 145 reason good enough.

Mar. The devil a Puritan that he is, or anything constantly but a time-pleaser; an affectioned ass, that cons state without book and utters it by great swarths; the best persuaded of himself; so crammed, 150 as he thinks, with excellencies that it is his grounds of faith that all that look on him love him; and on that vice in him will my revenge find notable cause to work.

To. What wilt thou do? 155

Mar. I will drop in his way some obscure epistles of love, wherein by the color of his beard, the shape of his leg, the manner of his gait, the expressure of his eye, forehead, and complexion, he shall find himself most feelingly personated. I can write very like 160 my lady your niece; on a forgotten matter we can hardly make distinction of our hands.

To. Excellent! I smell a device.

And. I have't in my nose too.

To. He shall think by the letters that thou wilt 165 drop that they come from my niece, and that she's in love with him.

Mar. My purpose is indeed a horse of that color.

And. And your horse now would make him an ass.

Mar. Ass, I doubt not.

And. O, 'twill be admirable! 170

Mar. Sport royal, I warrant you. I know my physic

176. **on:** of; **event:** outcome.

177. **Penthesilea:** queen of the Amazons. Although small, Maria is doughty at this kind of warfare.

178. **Before me:** on my word; a casual oath.

184-85. **recover:** obtain possession of by legal means; i.e., marry; **a foul way out:** distressingly out of pocket, not only for routine expenses of courtship but for having loaned sums to Sir Toby. See III. ii. 54-5.

187. **Cut:** a horse (either dock-tailed or gelded). Horses were considered stupid and calling anyone a horse indicated contempt.

190. **burn some sack:** heat some sherry.

▪▪▪▪▪▪▪▪▪▪▪▪▪▪▪▪▪▪▪▪▪▪▪▪▪▪▪▪▪▪▪▪▪▪▪▪▪▪

II. iv. Orsino is languishing for Olivia and calls for a melancholy love-lament in tune with his mood. It is clear that he is more in love with love than with Olivia, but inspired by the song, he sends Cesario once more to press his suit. Cesario has confessed her own love for Orsino, but in terms that he does not understand.

▪▪▪▪▪▪▪▪▪▪▪▪▪▪▪▪▪▪▪▪▪▪▪▪▪▪▪▪▪▪

4. **antique:** old-fashioned.

will work with him. I will plant you two, and let the
fool make a third, where he shall find the letter. Observe his construction of it. For this night, to bed, 175
and dream on the event. Farewell.   *Exit.*

To. Good night, Penthesilea.

And. Before me, she's a good wench.

To. She's a beagle true-bred, and one that adores
me. What o' that?   180

And. I was adored once too.

To. Let's to bed, knight. Thou hadst need send for
more money.

And. If I cannot recover your niece, I am a foul
way out.   185

To. Send for money, knight. If thou hast her not i'
the end, call me Cut.

And. If I do not, never trust me, take it how you
will.

To. Come, come; I'll go burn some sack. 'Tis too 190
late to go to bed now. Come, knight; come, knight.
                                        Exeunt.

Scene IV. [The Duke's Palace.]

Enter *Duke, Viola, Curio,* and others.

Duke. Give me some music. Now good morrow,
    friends.
Now, good Cesario, but that piece of song,
That old and antique song we heard last night.

5. **passion:** suffering. The word was not confined to amorous emotions but was used for intense feelings of all sorts.

6. **recollected:** i.e., painstakingly brought together; the opposite of spontaneous and natural expression. What Orsino objects to in current airs is their affectation.

20. **motions:** i.e., things which have power to move him.

23-4. **It gives a very echo to the seat/ Where Love is throned:** it exactly echoes the heart of a lover.

27. **stayed:** rested; **favor:** face.

29. **by your favor:** a courteous expression: if you will have it so.

31. **complexion:** temperament, disposition.

Methought it did relieve my passion much, 5
More than light airs and recollected terms
Of these most brisk and giddy-paced times.
Come, but one verse.

Cur. He is not here, so please your lordship, that
should sing it. 10

Duke. Who was it?

Cur. Feste the jester, my lord, a fool that the Lady
Olivia's father took much delight in. He is about the
house.

Duke. Seek him out. [*Exit Curio.*] And play the 15
    tune the while. *Music plays.*
Come hither, boy. If ever thou shalt love,
In the sweet pangs of it remember me;
For such as I am all true lovers are,
Unstaid and skittish in all motions else 20
Save in the constant image of the creature
That is beloved. How dost thou like this tune?

Vio. It gives a very echo to the seat
Where Love is throned.

Duke.   Thou dost speak masterly. 25
My life upon't, young though thou art, thine eye
Hath stayed upon some favor that it loves.
Hath it not, boy?

Vio.   A little, by your favor.

Duke. What kind of woman is't? 30

Vio.   Of your complexion.

Duke. She is not worth thee then. What years, i'
    faith?

Vio. About your years, my lord.

35. **still:** ever, always.

37. **wears she to him:** she molds herself to his liking.

38. **sways she level in her husband's heart:** she retains her unaltered rule of her husband's heart.

40. **fancies:** love-fancies, amorous inclinations; see I. i. 14.

41. **won:** Thomas Hanmer's correction of the Folio "worne."

45. **hold the bent:** maintain the same pitch of ardor; remain stretched to its limit, like a bent bow.

53. **free:** carefree.

54. **bones:** bone bobbins, used in making bone lace.

55. **Do use:** are accustomed; **silly sooth:** unadorned truth. Silly means "simple."

56. **dallies:** plays.

57. **Like the old age:** in an old-fashioned way.

Duke. Too old, by heaven! Let still the woman   35
    take
An elder than herself: so wears she to him,
So sways she level in her husband's heart;
For, boy, however we do praise ourselves,
Our fancies are more giddy and unfirm,   40
More longing, wavering, sooner lost and won,
Than women's are.
    Vio.   I think it well, my lord.
    Duke. Then let thy love be younger than thyself,
Or thy affection cannot hold the bent;   45
For women are as roses, whose fair flower,
Being once displayed, doth fall that very hour.
    Vio. And so they are; alas, that they are so!
To die, even when they to perfection grow!

                Enter *Curio* and *Clown.*

    Duke. O, fellow, come, the song we had last night. 50
Mark it, Cesario; it is old and plain.
The spinsters and the knitters in the sun,
And the free maids that weave their thread with
    bones,
Do use to chant it. It is silly sooth,   55
And dallies with the innocence of love,
Like the old age.
    Clown. Are you ready, sir?
    Duke. Ay; prithee sing.   *Music.*

61. **sad:** dark in color, black; **cypress:** a coffin of cypress wood.

62. **Fly away, fly away:** Nicholas Rowe's correction. The Folios have "Fye . . . fie."

66-7. **My part of death, no one so true/ Did share it:** no one ever so faithfully embraced inevitable death as I do.

70. **greet:** lament.

80. **pleasure will be paid:** i.e., paid for.

84. **doublet:** jacket; the upper part of a man's suit.

85-6. **of such constancy:** that is, so little constancy, such changeability of mood.

The Song.

Clown. Come away, come away, death,   60
    And in sad cypress let me be laid.
Fly away, fly away, breath;
    I am slain by a fair cruel maid.
My shroud of white, stuck all with yew,
    O, prepare it!   65
My part of death, no one so true
    Did share it.

Not a flower, not a flower sweet,
    On my black coffin let there be strown;
Not a friend, not a friend greet   70
    My poor corpse, where my bones shall
    be thrown.
A thousand thousand sighs to save,
    Lay me, O, where
Sad true lover never find my grave,   75
    To weep there!

Duke. There's for thy pains.
Clown. No pains, sir. I take pleasure in singing, sir.
Duke. I'll pay thy pleasure then.
Clown. Truly, sir, and pleasure will be paid one   80
time or another.
Duke. Give me now leave to leave thee.
Clown. Now the melancholy god protect thee, and
the tailor make thy doublet of changeable taffeta, for
thy mind is a very opal! I would have men of such   85

87. intent: object, destination; **that's it:** a person of such constancy.

88. nothing: i.e., no settled purpose.

90. give place: clear away, leave.

92. sovereign cruelty: i.e., the cruel woman who rules me.

96. hold as giddily as Fortune: regard as indifferently as does the goddess Fortune, who bestowed them. Fortune was proverbially described as fickle and inclined to bestow her favors whimsically.

97-8. that miracle and queen of gems/ That nature pranks her in: the wondrous beauty of that body in which nature has dressed her.

107. bide: endure.

111. motion: movement; see l. 20; **liver:** the source of love, according to contemporary belief; see I. i. 39.

112. cloyment: satiation; **revolt:** revulsion, nausea.

constancy put to sea, that their business might be everything, and their intent everywhere; for that's it
that always makes a good voyage of nothing. Fare-
well.   *Exit*.

   Duke. Let all the rest give place.   90

                [*Exeunt Curio and Attendants*.]

                     Once more, Cesario,
Get thee to yond same sovereign cruelty.
Tell her, my love, more noble than the world,
Prizes not quantity of dirty lands.
The parts that Fortune hath bestowed upon her,   95
Tell her I hold as giddily as Fortune;
But 'tis that miracle and queen of gems
That nature pranks her in, attracts my soul.

   Vio. But if she cannot love you, sir—

   Duke. I cannot be so answered.   100

   Vio.   Sooth, but you must.
Say that some lady, as perhaps there is,
Hath for your love as great a pang of heart
As you have for Olivia: You cannot love her;
You tell her so. Must she not then be answered?   105

   Duke. There is no woman's sides
Can bide the beating of so strong a passion
As love doth give my heart; no woman's heart
So big to hold so much; they lack retention.
Alas, their love may be called appetite—   110
No motion of the liver, but the palate—
That suffers surfeit, cloyment, and revolt;
But mine is all as hungry as the sea
And can digest as much. Make no compare

127. damask: blended red and white; the comparison is with a damask rose; **thought:** melancholy.

132. Our shows are more than will: our pretense of love is greater than our actual desire; **still:** always; see l. 35.

137. to: a grammatical construction in which the verb "go" or an equivalent is understood.

140. denay: denial.

An English nobleman.
From Pietro Bertelli, *Diversarum nationum habitus* (1594).

Between that love a woman can bear me 115
And that I owe Olivia.
 Vio.   Ay, but I know—
 Duke. What dost thou know?
 Vio. Too well what love women to men may owe.
In faith, they are as true of heart as we. 120
My father had a daughter loved a man
As it might be perhaps, were I a woman,
I should your lordship.
 Duke.   And what's her history?
 Vio. A blank, my lord. She never told her love, 125
But let concealment, like a worm i' the bud,
Feed on her damask cheek. She pined in thought;
And, with a green and yellow melancholy,
She sat like Patience on a monument,
Smiling at grief. Was not this love indeed? 130
We men may say more, swear more; but indeed
Our shows are more than will; for still we prove
Much in our vows but little in our love.
 Duke. But died thy sister of her love, my boy?
 Vio. I am all the daughters of my father's house, 135
And all the brothers too—and yet I know not.
Sir, shall I to this lady?
 Duke.   Ay, that's the theme.
To her in haste! Give her this jewel. Say
My love can give no place, bide no denay. 140
         Exeunt.

II. v. Sir Toby, Sir Andrew, Maria, and Fabian, another member of Olivia's household, plot the downfall of Malvolio. Malvolio finds the planted letter, which hints at love for him and urges him to smile, to wear yellow stockings and cross-garters, and to be haughty and distant to Sir Toby. Malvolio, to the delight of his observers, is taken in and gloats in anticipation of his good fortune. As he goes off, musing at the glory that is to be his, the conspirators congratulate themselves and look forward to his reception when he approaches Olivia, all smiles, wearing the yellow stockings and foppish cross-garters that she detests.

▪▪▪▪▪▪▪▪▪▪▪▪▪▪▪▪▪▪▪▪▪▪▪▪▪▪▪▪▪

2. **scruple:** little bit.

5. **sheepbiter:** a dog that bites sheep, later a petty thief; i.e., a sneak.

13. **metal of India:** a phrase meaning "gold," used by Sir Toby here in admiration of Maria's value as a trickster.

19. **Close:** keep close (hidden).

Scene V. [Olivia's garden.]

Enter Sir *Toby*, Sir *Andrew*, and *Fabian*.

To. Come thy ways, Signior Fabian.

Fab. Nay, I'll come. If I lose a scruple of this
sport, let me be boiled to death with melancholy.

To. Wouldst thou not be glad to have the niggard-
ly rascally sheepbiter come by some notable shame? 5

Fab. I would exult, man. You know he brought me
out o' favor with my lady about a bear-baiting here.

To. To anger him we'll have the bear again; and
we will fool him black and blue. Shall we not, Sir
Andrew? 10

And. An we do not, it is pity of our lives.

Enter *Maria*.

To. Here comes the little villain. How now, my
metal of India?

Mar. Get ye all three into the box tree. Malvolio's
coming down this walk. He has been yonder i' the 15
sun practicing behavior to his own shadow this half
hour. Observe him, for the love of mockery; for I
know this letter will make a contemplative idiot of
him. Close, in the name of jesting! Lie thou there
[*Throws down a letter*]; for here comes the trout 20
that must be caught with tickling. *Exit.*

23. **affect:** incline toward; like.

25. **complexion:** temperament; see II. iv. 31.

26-7. **follows her:** that is, in the capacity of a servant or retainer; **on't:** of it.

28. **overweening:** conceited.

30. **jets:** swaggers.

31. **'Slight:** a contraction of "by God's light."

37-8. **The Lady of the Strachy:** this phrase has caused endless comment among Shakespeare editors who have attempted to explain it. No one has yet found a satisfactory explanation of this allusion.

39. **Jezebel:** a biblical character (I and II Kings) whose pride led to her destruction.

41. **blows:** swells.

43. **state:** chair of state.

44. **stonebow:** a crossbow which propelled stones, used in fowling.

45. **branched:** patterned, probably in branches and foliage.

Jezebel.

From Guillaume Rouille, *Del prontuario de le medaglie de piu illustri, & fulgenti huomini & donne* (1553).

41

Enter *Malvolio*.

Mal. 'Tis but fortune; all is fortune. Maria once told me she did affect me; and I have heard herself come thus near, that, should she fancy, it should be one of my complexion. Besides, she uses me with a 25 more exalted respect than anyone else that follows her. What should I think on't?

To. Here's an overweening rogue!

Fab. O, peace! Contemplation makes a rare turkey cock of him. How he jets under his advanced plumes! 30

And. 'Slight, I could so beat the rogue!

Fab. Peace, I say.

Mal. To be Count Malvolio!

To. Ah, rogue!

And. Pistol him, pistol him! 35

Fab. Peace, peace!

Mal. There is example for't. The Lady of the Strachy married the yeoman of the wardrobe.

And. Fie on him, Jezebel!

Fab. O, peace! Now he's deeply in. Look how 40 imagination blows him.

Mal. Having been three months married to her, sitting in my state—

To. O for a stonebow, to hit him in the eye!

Mal. Calling my officers about me, in my branched 45 velvet gown; having come from a day bed, where I have left Olivia sleeping—

To. Fire and brimstone!

Fab. O, peace, peace!

50. **to have the humor of state:** to give expression to the dignity of my position.

51. **after a demure travel of regard:** after surveying the assembly in a reserved manner.

57. **make out for him:** set out to fetch him.

64. **an austere regard of control:** a severe look of mastery.

65. **take:** i.e., give.

72. **scab:** scurvy fellow.

Mal. And then to have the humor of state; and   50
after a demure travel of regard—telling them I know
my place, as I would they should do theirs—to ask for
my kinsman Toby—

To. Bolts and shackles!

Fab. O, peace, peace, peace! Now, now.   55

Mal. Seven of my people, with an obedient start,
make out for him. I frown the while, and perchance
wind up my watch, or play with my—some rich jewel.
Toby approaches; curtsies there to me—

To. Shall this fellow live?   60

Fab. Though our silence be drawn from us with
cars, yet peace!

Mal. I extend my hand to him thus, quenching my
familiar smile with an austere regard of control—

To. And does not Toby take you a blow o' the lips   65
then?

Mal. Saying, "Cousin Toby, my fortunes having
cast me on your niece, give me this prerogative of
speech."

To. What, what?   70

Mal. "You must amend your drunkenness."

To. Out, scab!

Fab. Nay, patience, or we break the sinews of our
plot.

Mal. "Besides, you waste the treasure of your time   75
with a foolish knight"—

And. That's me, I warrant you.

Mal. "One Sir Andrew"—

And. I knew 'twas I, for many do call me fool.

81. **woodcock:** traditionally a fowl that was easily tricked, and the word by extension became synonymous with fool; **gin:** snare, trap.

82. **the spirit of humors:** the controller of impulse.

90-1. **By your leave, wax:** Malvolio apologizes to the wax seal before breaking it; **her Lucrece:** Lucrece, noted for her chastity, was apparently the symbol adopted by Olivia as a seal.

94. **liver and all:** i.e., he is not only completely fooled into thinking that the letter is from Olivia, but already on the way to feeling a passion for her in return; see **liver,** II. iv. 111.

99-100. **The numbers altered:** different versification.

102. **brock:** badger; by extension, a dirty and stinking fellow.

106. **sway:** rule; see II. iv. 38.

107. **fustian riddle:** i.e., gibberish.

Lucrece.

From Guillaume Rouille, *Del prontuario de le medaglie de piu illustri, & fulgenti huomini & donne* (1553).

Mal. What employment have we here?   80

[*Picks up the letter.*]

Fab. Now is the woodcock near the gin.

To. O, peace! and the spirit of humors intimate reading aloud to him!

Mal. By my life, this is my lady's hand! These be her very C's, her U's, and her T's; and thus makes   85
she her great P's. It is, in contempt of question, her hand.

And. Her C's, her U's, and her T's? Why that?

Mal. [*Reads*] "To the unknown beloved, this, and my good wishes." Her very phrases! By your leave,   90
wax. Soft! and the impressure her Lucrece, with which she uses to seal! 'Tis my lady. To whom should this be?

Fab. This wins him, liver and all.

Mal. [*Reads*]

> "Jove knows I love—   95
>   But who?
> Lips, do not move;
>   No man must know."

"No man must know." What follows? The numbers altered! "No man must know." If this should be thee,   100
Malvolio?

To. Marry, hang thee, brock!

Mal. [*Reads*]

> "I may command where I adore;
>   But silence, like a Lucrece knife,
> With bloodless stroke my heart doth gore.   105
>   M. O. A. I. doth sway my life."

Fab. A fustian riddle!

111. **dressed:** prepared.

112. **staniel:** Hanmer's correction of the Folio reading "stallion." A **staniel** is a variety of hawk; **checks:** pursues a false quarry; a technical term from falconry.

115-16. **formal capacity:** sane understanding; **obstruction:** difficulty.

119. **make up:** put together in sensible fashion; interpret.

120-21. **Sowter will cry upon't for all this, though it be as rank as a fox:** this bungling dog will pursue his quarry though it should be obvious that he is being tricked. **Sowter** literally means a cobbler, i.e., a bungler.

125. **excellent at faults:** i.e., he can make something intelligible that will suit his notions out of the most senseless set of clues. **Fault** is a hunting term meaning an interruption of the scent or a loss of the quarry.

126. **consonancy:** consistency.

127. **suffers under probation:** i.e., will not bear close examination.

129. **O shall end, I hope:** Malvolio's discomfiture will be the outcome. **O** was sometimes used as a noun meaning the equivalent of lamentation.

135-37. **This simulation is not as the former:** this disguised message is not as clear as the previous phrase; **to crush this a little, it would bow to me:** with a little pressure I can force this disordered set of letters into my name.

To. Excellent wench, say I.

Mal. "M. O. A. I. doth sway my life." Nay, but first, let me see, let me see, let me see.   110

Fab. What dish o' poison has she dressed him!

To. And with what wing the staniel checks at it!

Mal. "I may command where I adore." Why, she may command me: I serve her; she is my lady. Why, this is evident to any formal capacity. There is no ob- 115 struction in this. And the end—what should that alphabetical position portend? If I could make that resemble something in me! Softly! M. O. A. I.

To. O, ay, make up that! He is now at a cold scent.

Fab. Sowter will cry upon't for all this, though it 120 be as rank as a fox.

Mal. M.—Malvolio. M.—Why, that begins my name!

Fab. Did not I say he would work it out? The cur is excellent at faults.   125

Mal. M.—But then there is no consonancy in the sequel. That suffers under probation. A should follow, but O does.

Fab. And O shall end, I hope.

To. Ay, or I'll cudgel him, and make him cry O! 130

Mal. And then I comes behind.

Fab. Ay, an you had any eye behind you, you might see more detraction at your heels than fortunes before you.

Mal. M, O, A, I. This simulation is not as the for- 135 mer; and yet, to crush this a little, it would bow to me, for every one of these letters are in my name. Soft! here follows prose.

139. **revolve:** consider.

140. **stars:** i.e., birth, destiny.

144-45. **inure:** accustom; **like:** likely; **cast thy humble slough:** discard thy lowly trappings, as a snake discards its old skin.

146-48. **Let thy tongue tang arguments of state:** discourse of statesmanlike matters; **put thyself into the trick of singularity:** adopt the habit of behaving in an individual manner.

150. **cross-gartered:** wearing ribbon garters which crossed in back of the knee and tied in a large bow above the knee in front.

154. **alter services:** exchange roles, assuming his subordinate position to be ruled by him.

156. **champian:** flat and open country; **discovers:** reveals.

157. **politic authors:** authors wise in statecraft—in order to be able to talk learnedly on the subject as advised in the letter.

158. **baffle:** disgrace publicly; treat with contempt before others.

159. **point-device:** in every point, perfectly.

160. **jade me:** behave like a jade to me; trick me.

161. **excites to this:** i.e., prompts this belief.

164. **manifests herself to my love:** reveals her desire for my love.

165. **these habits of her liking:** these articles of clothing which please her.

166. **happy:** lucky; **strange:** stern and aloof; **stout:** arrogant.

[*Reads*] "If this fall into thy hand, revolve. In my
stars I am above thee; but be not afraid of greatness. 140
Some are born great, some achieve greatness, and
some have greatness thrust upon 'em. Thy Fates open
their hands; let thy blood and spirit embrace them;
and to inure thyself to what thou art like to be, cast
thy humble slough and appear fresh. Be opposite 145
with a kinsman, surly with servants. Let thy tongue
tang arguments of state; put thyself into the trick of
singularity. She thus advises thee that sighs for thee.
Remember who commended thy yellow stockings
and wished to see thee ever cross-gartered. I say, re- 150
member. Go to, thou art made, if thou desirest to be
so. If not, let me see thee a steward still, the fellow
of servants, and not worthy to touch Fortune's fingers.
Farewell. She that would alter services with thee,

                    "THE FORTUNATE UNHAPPY." 155

Daylight and champian discovers not more. This is
open. I will be proud, I will read politic authors, I
will baffle Sir Toby, I will wash off gross acquaintance, I will be point-device the very man. I do not
now fool myself, to let imagination jade me; for ev- 160
ery reason excites to this, that my lady loves me. She
did commend my yellow stockings of late, she did
praise my leg being cross-gartered; and in this she
manifests herself to my love, and with a kind of in-
junction drives me to these habits of her liking. I 165
thank my stars, I am happy. I will be strange, stout,
in yellow stockings, and cross-gartered, even with

171. **entertainst:** welcomest; see **entertainment,** I. v. 218 and II. i. 32.

173. **still:** always; see II. iv. 35 and II. iv. 132.

177. **the Sophy:** the Shah of Persia.

183. **gull-catcher:** catcher of fools; see **gull,** II. iii. 136.

186. **tray-trip:** a dice game.

192. **aqua vitae:** liquor.

The Sophy of Persia.

From Guillaume Rouille, *Del prontuario de le medaglie de piu illustri, & fulgenti huomini & donne* (1553).

the swiftness of putting on. Jove and my stars be
praised! Here is yet a postscript.

"Thou canst not choose but know who I am. If thou 170
entertainst my love, let it appear in thy smiling. Thy
smiles become thee well. Therefore in my presence
still smile, dear my sweet, I prithee."

Jove, I thank thee. I will smile; I will do everything
that thou wilt have me.   *Exit.* 175

Fab. I will not give my part of this sport for a pen-
sion of thousands to be paid from the Sophy.

To. I could marry this wench for this device—
And. So could I too.

To. And ask no other dowry with her but such an- 180
other jest.

Enter *Maria.*

And. Nor I neither.
Fab. Here comes my noble gull-catcher.
To. Wilt thou set thy foot o' my neck?
And. Or o' mine either?   185
To. Shall I play my freedom at tray-trip and be-
come thy bondslave?
And. I' faith, or I either?
To. Why, thou hast put him in such a dream that,
when the image of it leaves him, he must run mad. 190
Mar. Nay, but say true, does it work upon him?
To. Like aqua vitae with a midwife.
Mar. If you will, then, see the fruits of the sport,

201. Tartar: Tartarus, the infernal regions.
203. make one: go along.

A hearty Elizabethan of the type of Sir Toby Belch.
From a broadside ballad in the Roxburghe Collection.

mark his first approach before my lady. He will come to her in yellow stockings, and 'tis a color she abhors, 195 and cross-gartered, a fashion she detests; and he will smile upon her, which will now be so unsuitable to her disposition, being addicted to a melancholy as she is, that it cannot but turn him into a notable contempt. If you will see it, follow me. 200

To. To the gates of Tartar, thou most excellent devil of wit!

And. I'll make one too.

Exeunt.

TWELFTH NIGHT

ACT III

III. i. Cesario returns to renew Orsino's suit to Olivia and the latter hints at her love for his messenger. Cesario is properly distant, but Olivia bids him come again with the promise that his pleading may move her to Orsino's cause.

Ent. **tabor:** a small drum.
5. **No such matter:** not at all.
11. **You have said:** well said.
12. **chev'ril:** flexible kidskin.
14. **dally nicely:** play lasciviously.

ACT III

Scene I. [Olivia's garden.]

Enter Viola, and Clown [with a tabor and pipe].

Vio. Save thee, friend, and thy music! Dost thou live by thy tabor?

Clown. No, sir, I live by the church.

Vio. Art thou a churchman?

Clown. No such matter, sir. I do live by the church; for I do live at my house, and my house doth stand by the church. 5

Vio. So thou mayst say, the king lies by a beggar, if a beggar dwell near him; or, the church stands by thy tabor, if thy tabor stand by the church. 10

Clown. You have said, sir. To see this age! A sentence is but a chev'ril glove to a good wit. How quickly the wrong side may be turned outward!

Vio. Nay, that's certain. They that dally nicely with words may quickly make them wanton. 15

Clown. I would therefore my sister had had no name, sir.

Vio. Why, man?

Clown. Why, sir, her name's a word, and to dally with that word might make my sister wanton. But in- 20

48

21-2. since bonds disgraced them: since a bond is now considered necessary, a man's word no longer being sufficient assurance of his honesty.

29-30. in my conscience: as conscience is my judge.

36. pilchards: small fish related to the herring.

39. late: recently; see I. ii. 32.

40. the orb: this globe, the earth.

41-2. I would be sorry . . . but the fool should be: I would be sorry if the fool were not. In other words, the Clown would not like it said that his mistress was more foolish than the Duke.

43. your wisdom: an ironical title.

44. pass upon: as though in fencing; in other words, a verbal duel.

46. commodity: consignment.

48-9. sick for one: i.e., for lack of the man I love.

deed words are very rascals since bonds disgraced
them.

Vio. Thy reason, man?

Clown. Troth, sir, I can yield you none without
words, and words are grown so false I am loath to   25
prove reason with them.

Vio. I warrant thou art a merry fellow and carest
for nothing.

Clown. Not so, sir; I do care for something; but in
my conscience, sir, I do not care for you. If that be to   30
care for nothing, sir, I would it would make you invisible.

Vio. Art not thou the Lady Olivia's fool?

Clown. No, indeed, sir. The Lady Olivia has no
folly. She will keep no fool, sir, till she be married;   35
and fools are as like husbands as pilchards are to her-
rings—the husband's the bigger. I am indeed not her
fool, but her corrupter of words.

Vio. I saw thee late at the Count Orsino's.

Clown. Foolery, sir, does walk about the orb like   40
the sun; it shines everywhere. I would be sorry, sir,
but the fool should be as oft with your master as
with my mistress. I think I saw your wisdom there.

Vio. Nay, an thou pass upon me, I'll no more with
thee. Hold, there's expenses for thee.   45

[*Gives a piece of money.*]

Clown. Now Jove, in his next commodity of hair,
send thee a beard!

Vio. By my troth, I'll tell thee, I am almost sick
for one, though I would not have it grow on my chin.
Is thy lady within?   50

51. **a pair of these:** the Clown holds up the coin which Cesario has given him and hints for another.

52. **use:** lending at interest.

53. **Pandarus:** the uncle of Cressida, who fostered Troilus' suit with her.

56-7. **begging but a beggar:** Feste has begged for a Cressida and that lady in Robert Henryson's *Testament of Cressid* ended as a leprous beggar.

59. **conster:** explain.

60. **welkin:** heavens; see II. iii. 57.

61. **element:** another name for "heavens"; see I. i. 28.

63. **craves:** requires; **wit:** intelligence.

66. **the haggard:** an untamed hawk; **check at:** pursue; see II. v. 112.

67. **practice:** craft.

69. **wisely:** i.e., because he gains a living by it; **fit:** suitable.

70. **taint:** tarnish; **wit:** wisdom; see l. 63.

73. **Dieu vous garde, monsieur:** God save you, sir.

74. **Et vous aussi; votre serviteur:** and you also; your servant.

76. **encounter:** high-flown language inviting Cesario to enter.

77. **trade:** business.

79. **list:** end; literally, border of fabric.

Clown. Would not a pair of these have bred, sir?

Vio. Yes, being kept together and put to use.

Clown. I would play Lord Pandarus of Phrygia,
sir, to bring a Cressida to this Troilus.

Vio. I understand you, sir. 'Tis well begged.   55

Clown. The matter, I hope, is not great, sir, begging but a beggar: Cressida was a beggar. [*Viola
tosses him another coin.*] My lady is within, sir. I
will conster to them whence you come. Who you are
and what you would are out of my welkin—I might   60
say "element," but the word is over-worn.   *Exit.*

Vio. This fellow is wise enough to play the fool,
And to do that well craves a kind of wit.
He must observe their mood on whom he jests,
The quality of persons, and the time;   65
Not, like the haggard, check at every feather
That comes before his eye. This is a practice
As full of labor as a wise man's art;
For folly that he wisely shows, is fit;
But wise men, folly-fall'n, quite taint their wit.   70

Enter *Sir Toby* and [*Sir*] *Andrew.*

To. Save you, gentleman!

Vio. And you, sir.

And. Dieu vous garde, monsieur.

Vio. Et vous aussi; votre serviteur.

And. I hope, sir, you are, and I am yours.   75

To. Will you encounter the house? My niece is
desirous you should enter, if your trade be to her.

Vio. I am bound to your niece, sir. I mean, she is
the list of my voyage.

81. understand me: the pun should be obvious.

86. prevented: forestalled.

91-2. My matter hath no voice, lady, but to your own most pregnant and vouchsafed ear: my message is only for your ready and proffered ear.

94. I'll get 'em all three all ready: Sir Andrew means that he will learn these three elegant words so he can use them as casually as Cesario has done.

102. lowly feigning was called compliment: i.e., pretense of being another's servant for the sake of formal courtesy. Olivia, in love with Cesario, would like the youth to be her servant as a lover is that of his adored mistress.

104. his: that is, all that is his.

A haggard falcon.
From Gervase Markham, *Hunger's Prevention, or, The Whole Art of Fowling* (1655).

51

To. Taste your legs, sir; put them to motion.   80

- *Vio.* My legs do better understand me, sir, than I understand what you mean by bidding me taste my legs.

To. I mean, to go, sir, to enter.

Vio. I will answer you with gait and entrance.   85
But we are prevented.

Enter *Olivia* and *Gentlewoman* [*Maria*].

Most excellent accomplished lady, the heavens rain odors on you!

And. [*Aside*] That youth's a rare courtier. "Rain odors"—well!   90

Vio. My matter hath no voice, lady, but to your own most pregnant and vouchsafed ear.

And. [*Aside*] "Odors," "pregnant," and "vouchsafed"—I'll get 'em all three all ready.

Oli. Let the garden door be shut, and leave me to   95
my hearing. [*Exeunt Sir Toby, Sir Andrew, and Maria.*] Give me your hand, sir.

Vio. My duty, madam, and most humble service.

Oli. What is your name?

Vio. Cesario is your servant's name, fair princess.   100

Oli. My servant, sir? 'Twas never merry world
Since lowly feigning was called compliment.
Y'are servant to the Count Orsino, youth.

Vio. And he is yours, and his must needs be yours.
Your servant's servant is your servant, madam.   105

Oli. For him, I think not on him; for his thoughts,
Would they were blanks, rather than filled with me!

118. **abuse:** deceive.

120. **Under your hard construction must I sit:** you must have a poor opinion of me.

124-25. **set . . . at the stake/ And baited:** Olivia uses an image from the sport of bear-baiting, which consisted of tying a bear to a stake and setting on it fierce mastiff dogs which had been trained to attack it.

126-27. **tyrannous:** fierce, uncontrollable; **receiving:** understanding.

128: **cypress:** a transparent silk fabric used for scarves and veils, so called because originally imported from Cyprus.

131. **degree:** step or stage.

132. **grise:** synonymous with **degree;** **'tis a vulgar proof:** that is, something proved by common experience.

134. **'tis time to smile again:** i.e., if Cesario hates her, Olivia should then cast off her lovesick longing and be cheerful again.

136-37. **better/ To fall before the lion than the wolf:** the lion is at least king of beasts, the wolf inferior to him. Olivia means that it would be better to have her heart fall to a noble and courtly lover like Orsino rather than a heartless and inferior young man.

Vio. Madam, I come to whet your gentle thoughts
On his behalf.

Oli.   O, by your leave, I pray you!   110
I bade you never speak again of him;
But, would you undertake another suit,
I had rather hear you to solicit that
Than music from the spheres.

Vio.   Dear lady—   115

Oli. Give me leave, beseech you. I did send,
After the last enchantment you did here,
A ring in chase of you. So did I abuse
Myself, my servant, and, I fear me, you.
Under your hard construction must I sit,   120
To force that on you in a shameful cunning
Which you knew none of yours. What might you
        think?
Have you not set mine honor at the stake
And baited it with all the unmuzzled thoughts   125
That tyrannous heart can think? To one of your re-
        ceiving
Enough is shown; a cypress, not a bosom,
Hides my heart. So, let me hear you speak.

Vio. I pity you.   130

Oli.   That's a degree to love.

Vio. No, not a grise; for 'tis a vulgar proof
That very oft we pity enemies.

Oli. Why then, methinks 'tis time to smile again.
O world, how apt the poor are to be proud!   135
If one should be a prey, how much the better
To fall before the lion than the wolf!

                        Clock strikes.

140. **is come to harvest:** have matured.

141. **proper:** fine, handsome; see II. ii. 29.

143. **westward ho:** the call used to summon a boatman for a westward passage on the Thames. Travel through the narrow London streets was so unpleasant that the Thames was a popular route from one part of the city to another.

145. **nothing:** i.e., send no message.

148. **you do think you are not what you are:** i.e., you think you are the rejected lover of a man, when I am a woman.

149. **I think the same of you:** Olivia understands Cesario to mean that she is deluded and replies that Cesario must also lack judgment to reject her love.

153. **I am your fool:** as balm to Olivia's feelings she can interpret this to mean that she is joking, but the real meaning is that Olivia's offer of love is an embarrassment.

157. **night is noon:** that is, it shines as brightly at night as at noon; it cannot be hidden.

160. **maugre:** despite; **pride:** proud disdain of me.

162-65. **Do . . . better:** do not conclude because I offer myself unasked that I am not worth wooing, but instead put one factor with the other and conclude that freely offered love is better than love which has been arduously solicited.

The clock upbraids me with the waste of time.
Be not afraid, good youth, I will not have you;
And yet, when wit and youth is come to harvest,   140
Your wife is like to reap a proper man.
There lies your way, due west.

Vio.   Then westward ho!
Grace and good disposition attend your ladyship!
You'll nothing, madam, to my lord by me?   145

    Oli. Stay.
I prithee tell me what thou thinkst of me.

    Vio. That you do think you are not what you are.

    Oli. If I think so, I think the same of you.

    Vio. Then think you right. I am not what I am.   150

    Oli. I would you were as I would have you be!

    Vio. Would it be better, madam, than I am?
I wish it might; for now I am your fool.

    Oli. O, what a deal of scorn looks beautiful
In the contempt and anger of his lip!   155
A murd'rous guilt shows not itself more soon
Than love that would seem hid: love's night is noon.
Cesario, by the roses of the spring,
By maidhood, honor, truth, and everything,
I love thee so that, maugre all thy pride,   160
Nor wit nor reason can my passion hide.
Do not extort thy reasons from this clause,
For that I woo, thou therefore hast no cause;
But rather reason thus with reason fetter:
Love sought is good, but given unsought is better.   165

    Vio. By innocence I swear, and by my youth,
I have one heart, one bosom, and one truth,
And that no woman has; nor never none

III. ii. Sir Andrew, having seen Olivia showing more favor to Orsino's messenger than she has ever shown him, grows restive, but Sir Toby persuades him that Olivia was acting thus to make him jealous. Sir Toby also suggests that his rival should have aroused his valor and Sir Andrew agrees to write a challenge to the youth. In the meantime, Malvolio has followed the instructions of the letter and Maria reports that he is dressed in the prescribed stockings and garters, smiling idiotically. Sir Toby delightedly follows her to observe this phenomenon.

13. **'Slight:** by God's light; see II. v. 31.
14. **legitimate:** in a legal manner.

Shall mistress be of it, save I alone.
And so adieu, good madam. Never more 170
Will I my master's tears to you deplore.

Oli. Yet come again; for thou perhaps mayst move
That heart which now abhors to like his love.

Exeunt.

Scene II. [Olivia's house.]

Enter *Sir Toby, Sir Andrew,* and *Fabian.*

And. No, faith, I'll not stay a jot longer.

To. Thy reason, dear venom; give thy reason.

Fab. You must needs yield your reason, Sir Andrew.

And. Marry, I saw your niece do more favors to 5
the Count's servingman than ever she bestowed upon
me. I saw't i' the orchard.

To. Did she see thee the while, old boy? Tell me
that.

And. As plain as I see you now. 10

Fab. This was a great argument of love in her toward you.

And. 'Slight! will you make an ass o' me?

Fab. I will prove it legitimate, sir, upon the oaths
of judgment and reason. 15

To. And they have been grand-jurymen since before Noah was a sailor.

Fab. She did show favor to the youth in your sight

20-1. brimstone in your liver: to heat the source of passion.

24. balked: passed up.

29. policy: craft.

31. a Brownist: a member of a puritanical sect founded by Robert Browne.

42. curst: disagreeable, cross.

44. with the license of ink: as freely as pen can write.

45. thou'st: call him "thou," the pronoun used only to intimates and inferiors.

47-8. the bed of Ware: a tremendous four-poster bed, famous in this period and now preserved in the Victoria and Albert Museum in London.

only to exasperate you, to awake your dormouse
valor, to put fire in your heart and brimstone in your   20
liver. You should then have accosted her; and with
some excellent jests, fire-new from the mint, you
should have banged the youth into dumbness. This
was looked for at your hand, and this was balked.
The double gilt of this opportunity you let time wash   25
off, and you are now sailed into the North of my
lady's opinion, where you will hang like an icicle on
a Dutchman's beard unless you do redeem it by some
laudable attempt either of valor or policy.

And. An't be any way, it must be with valor; for   30
policy I hate. I had as lief be a Brownist as a poli-
tician.

To. Why then, build me thy fortunes upon the
basis of valor. Challenge me the Count's youth to
fight with him; hurt him in eleven places. My niece   35
shall take note of it; and assure thyself there is no
love-broker in the world can more prevail in man's
commendation with woman than report of valor.

Fab. There is no way but this, Sir Andrew.

And. Will either of you bear me a challenge to   40
him?

To. Go, write it in a martial hand. Be curst and
brief; it is no matter how witty, so it be eloquent and
full of invention. Taunt him with the license of ink.
If thou thou'st him some thrice, it shall not be amiss;   45
and as many lies as will lie in thy sheet of paper, although the sheet were big enough for the bed of
Ware in England, set 'em down. Go, about it! Let

49-50. though thou write with a goose-pen:
that is, writing with a goose quill should not make
your style foolish and timid.

52. cubiculo: presumably "cubicle." Sir Toby
probably means Sir Andrew's private chamber.

53. a dear manikin: a favorite plaything.

54. dear: expensive. Sir Toby means that he has
borrowed the sum mentioned, which Sir Andrew
has advanced on the expectation of marrying Olivia
and getting her fortune.

59. wainropes: wagon ropes.

61. blood in his liver: i.e., he is lily-livered
(cowardly).

64. opposite: opponent.

65. presage: presentiment, threat.

66. the youngest wren of mine: an affectionate
reference to Maria. Lewis Theobald corrected *mine*
to "nine" and since that time Shakespeare scholars
have learnedly discussed this as evidence of Shakespeare's observation of the wren's habit of laying a
large clutch of eggs and have concluded that he was
a learned ornithologist.

67. the spleen: the organ supposed to produce
fits of laughter.

69. renegado: renegade, apostate.

71-2. such impossible passages of grossness:
such obviously impossible notions as the letter expressed.

there be gall enough in thy ink, though thou write
with a goose-pen, no matter. About it!   **50**

And. Where shall I find you?

To. We'll call thee at the cubiculo. Go.

                                Exit Sir Andrew.

Fab. This is a dear manikin to you, Sir Toby.

To. I have been dear to him, lad—some two thousand strong, or so.   **55**

Fab. We shall have a rare letter from him—but
you'll not deliver't?

To. Never trust me then; and by all means stir on
the youth to an answer. I think oxen and wainropes
cannot hale them together. For Andrew, if he were   **60**
opened, and you find so much blood in his liver as
will clog the foot of a flea, I'll eat the rest of the
anatomy.

Fab. And his opposite, the youth, bears in his vis-
age no great presage of cruelty.   **65**

Enter *Maria.*

To. Look where the youngest wren of mine comes.

Mar. If you desire the spleen, and will laugh yourselves into stitches, follow me. Yond gull Malvolio
is turned heathen, a very renegado; for there is no
Christian that means to be saved by believing right-   **70**
ly can ever believe such impossible passages of grossness. He's in yellow stockings!

To. And cross-gartered?

Mar. Most villainously; like a pedant that keeps
a school i' the church. I have dogged him like his   **75**

78-9. the new map with the augmentation of the Indies: probably Edward Wright's map, which was printed in Richard Hakluyt's *Principal Navigations* (1598-1600).

III. iii. Antonio has overtaken Sebastian but, reluctant to be seen in the streets of Orsino's dukedom, he gives the youth his purse in case of need while he himself goes to engage rooms and order food at an inn called the Elephant.

8. jealousy: anxiety.

murderer. He does obey every point of the letter
that I dropped to betray him. He does smile his face
into more lines than is in the new map with the augmentation of the Indies. You have not seen such a
thing as 'tis. I can hardly forbear hurling things at   80
him. I know my lady will strike him. If she do, he'll
smile, and take't for a great favor.

To. Come bring us, bring us where he is!

Exeunt omnes.

Scene III. [A street.]

Enter *Sebastian* and *Antonio.*

Seb. I would not by my will have troubled you;
But since you make your pleasure of your pains,
I will no further chide you.

Ant. I could not stay behind you. My desire,
More sharp than filed steel, did spur me forth;   5
And not all love to see you (though so much
As might have drawn one to a longer voyage)
But jealousy what might befall your travel,
Being skilless in these parts; which to a stranger,
Unguided and unfriended, often prove   10
Rough and unhospitable. My willing love,
The rather by these arguments of fear,
Set forth in your pursuit.

Seb.   My kind Antonio,
I can no other answer make but thanks,   15

16. **ever thanks and oft:** thanks and is an addition by Theobald; the Folio reads "ever oft."

17. **uncurrent:** not negotiable.

18. **worth:** i.e., in monetary terms.

25. **renown:** bring renown to.

30. **it would scarce be answered:** he would be unable to satisfy the Duke for his previous conduct.

36. **for traffic's sake:** that is, in order that peaceful trade might continue.

38. **lapsed:** caught unawares.

42. **the Elephant:** an inn.

43. **bespeak our diet:** order our food.

46. **There shall you have me:** i.e., you can find me at the Elephant.

And thanks, and ever thanks; and oft good turns
Are shuffled off with such uncurrent pay.
But, were my worth as is my conscience firm,
You should find better dealing. What's to do?
Shall we go see the relics of this town?   20

  Ant. Tomorrow, sir; best first go see your lodging.

  Seb. I am not weary, and 'tis long to night.
I pray you let us satisfy our eyes
With the memorials and the things of fame
That do renown this city.   25

  Ant.   Would you'ld pardon me.
I do not without danger walk these streets.
Once in a sea-fight 'gainst the Count his galleys
I did some service; of such note indeed
That, were I ta'en here, it would scarce be answered.   30

  Seb. Belike you slew great number of his people?

  Ant. The offense is not of such a bloody nature,
Albeit the quality of the time and quarrel
Might well have given us bloody argument.
It might have since been answered in repaying   35
What we took from them, which for traffic's sake
Most of our city did. Only myself stood out;
For which, if I be lapsed in this place,
I shall pay dear.

  Seb.   Do not then walk too open.   40

  Ant. It doth not fit me. Hold, sir, here's my purse.
In the south suburbs at the Elephant
Is best to lodge. I will bespeak our diet,
Whiles you beguile the time and feed your knowl-
    edge   45
With viewing of the town. There shall you have me.

48. **toy:** trifle.

49-50. **your store/ . . . is not for idle markets:** your resources are insufficient for frivolous buying.

─────────────────────────────────

III. iv. Olivia has sent for Cesario and while waiting decides that a conversation with her grave and solemn steward will please her. When Malvolio enters in his ridiculous costume and speaks in a way incomprehensible to her, she is amazed. Thinking him mad, she orders Maria to see that he is looked after. Malvolio, blind to her true reaction, is still convinced of her passion for him, and Sir Toby, Fabian, and Maria plan to have him tied in a dark room as an actual madman.

Sir Andrew has penned a foolish challenge and the arrival of Cesario soon gives opportunity for its presentation. Sir Toby warns Cesario of the ferocity of Sir Andrew and deludes Sir Andrew about the valor of the youth. Both are terrified of an encounter but cannot escape it. As they draw, Antonio enters and comes to Cesario's assistance, thinking she is Sebastian. Some officers of the Duke enter and take Antonio into custody. Antonio asks Cesario for his purse but Cesario denies his acquaintance and can only offer the little money she has, with the result that Antonio thinks his friend has betrayed him in his hour of need. Cesario, however, is left with food for thought since Antonio mentioned Sebastian's name, which revives a hope that he is alive and well.

─────────────────────────────────

2. **of:** on.
6. **sad and civil:** sober and decorous.
14. **in's:** in his.

59

Seb. Why I your purse?

Ant. Haply your eye shall light upon some toy
You have desire to purchase; and your store
I think is not for idle markets, sir.   50

Seb. I'll be your purse-bearer, and leave you for
An hour.

Ant.   To the Elephant.
Seb.   I do remember.

Exeunt.

Scene IV. [Olivia's garden.]

Enter *Olivia* and *Maria.*

Oli. I have sent after him; he says he'll come.
How shall I feast him? what bestow of him?
For youth is bought more oft than begged or bor-
    rowed.
I speak too loud.   5
Where is Malvolio? He is sad and civil,
And suits well for a servant with my fortunes.
Where is Malvolio?

Mar. He's coming, madam; but in very strange
manner. He is sure possessed, madam.   10

Oli. Why, what's the matter? Does he rave?

Mar. No, madam, he does nothing but smile. Your
ladyship were best to have some guard about you if
he come, for sure the man is tainted in's wits.

21. **upon a sad occasion:** for a serious matter.

25. **sonnet:** verse.

31-2. **Roman hand:** Italian handwriting.

38. **At your request:** Malvolio means that he is no more likely to condescend to answer the familiar questions of an inferior than the sweet-voiced nightingale would be likely to respond to a jackdaw's voice.

Oli. Go call him hither. [*Exit Maria.*] I am as mad   15
as he,
If sad and merry madness equal be.

Enter [*Maria,* with] *Malvolio.*

How now, Malvolio?
    Mal. Sweet lady, ho, ho!
    Oli. Smilest thou?   20
I sent for thee upon a sad occasion.
    Mal. Sad, lady? I could be sad. This does make
some obstruction in the blood, this cross-gartering;
but what of that? If it please the eye of one, it is
with me as the very true sonnet is, "Please one, and   25
please all."
    Oli. Why, how dost thou, man? What is the mat-
ter with thee?
    Mal. Not black in my mind, though yellow in my
legs. It did come to his hands, and commands shall   30
be executed. I think we do know the sweet Roman
hand.
    Oli. Wilt thou go to bed, Malvolio?
    Mal. To bed? Ay, sweetheart; and I'll come to thee.
    Oli. God comfort thee! Why dost thou smile so,   35
and kiss thy hand so oft?
    Mar. How do you, Malvolio?
    Mal. At your request? Yes, nightingales answer
daws!
    Mar. Why appear you with this ridiculous bold-   40
ness before my lady?
    Mal. "Be not afraid of greatness." 'Twas well writ.

59. very: veritable; see I. iii. 24; **midsummer madness:** midsummer was regarded as a time when antic behavior was common.

66. miscarry: come to harm.

68. come near me now: begin to understand my position.

Oli. What meanst thou by that, Malvolio?

Mal. "Some are born great"—

Oli. Ha?   45

Mal. "Some achieve greatness"—

Oli. What sayst thou?

Mal. "And some have greatness thrust upon them."

Oli. Heaven restore thee!

Mal. "Remember who commended thy yellow   50
stockings"—

Oli. Thy yellow stockings?

Mal. "And wished to see thee cross-gartered."

Oli. Cross-gartered?

Mal. "Go to, thou art made, if thou desirest to be   55
so"—

Oli. Am I made?

Mal. "If not, let me see thee a servant still."

Oli. Why, this is very midsummer madness.

Enter *Servant*.

Ser. Madam, the young gentleman of the Count   60
Orsino's is returned. I could hardly entreat him back.
He attends your ladyship's pleasure.

Oli. I'll come to him. [*Exit Servant.*] Good Maria,
let this fellow be looked to. Where's my cousin Toby?
Let some of my people have a special care of him. I   65
would not have him miscarry for the half of my
dowry.   *Exit* [*Olivia; then Maria*].

Mal. O ho! do you come near me now? No worse
man than Sir Toby to look to me! This concurs di-
rectly with the letter. She sends him on purpose,   70

71. **appear stubborn to him:** be firm with him.

77. **habit:** clothing; see II. v. 165.

78. **limed:** caught her in birdlime, a gluey substance used to trap small birds.

81. **degree:** station.

83. **dram of a scruple:** both **dram** and **scruple** were originally apothecaries' weights. In other words, "not the smallest thing."

84. **incredulous:** incredible; i.e., something beyond imagining.

89. **Legion:** a biblical allusion (Mark 5:9) to the man possessed by many devils.

93-4. **discard:** reject; will have nothing to do with; **private:** privacy.

that I may appear stubborn to him; for she incites
me to that in the letter. "Cast thy humble slough,"
says she; "be opposite with a kinsman, surly with
servants; let thy tongue tang with arguments of state;
put thyself into the trick of singularity";—and conse- 75
quently sets down the manner how: as, a sad face, a
reverend carriage, a slow tongue, in the habit of
some sir of note, and so forth. I have limed her; but
it is Jove's doing, and Jove make me thankful! And
when she went away now, "Let this fellow be looked 80
to." "Fellow!" not "Malvolio," nor after my degree,
but "fellow." Why, everything adheres together, that
no dram of a scruple, no scruple of a scruple, no ob-
stacle, no incredulous or unsafe circumstance—What
can be said? Nothing that can be can come between 85
me and the full prospect of my hopes. Well, Jove,
not I, is the doer of this, and he is to be thanked.

Enter [Sir] *Toby*, *Fabian*, and *Maria*.

To. Which way is he, in the name of sanctity? If
all the devils of hell be drawn in little, and Legion
himself possessed him, yet I'll speak to him. 90

Fab. Here he is, here he is! How is't with you, sir?
How is't with you, man?

Mal. Go off; I discard you. Let me enjoy my private. Go off.

Mar. Lo, how hollow the fiend speaks within him! 95
Did not I tell you? Sir Toby, my lady prays you to
have a care of him.

Mal. Aha! does she so?

100. **Let me alone:** let me deal with him; see II. iii. 135-36.

104. **La you:** lo, behold.

106. **water:** i.e., for urinalysis; **wise woman:** a "white witch" who dealt in beneficial magic such as healing with herbs.

113. **move:** stir up, excite.

117. **bawcock:** a term of affection.

118. **chuck:** another endearment.

120-21. **'tis not for gravity to play at cherry-pit with Satan:** a sober person like yourself should know better than to play games with the Devil. Cherry-pit was a child's game.

122. **collier:** i.e., Satan, because he is black. A collier is a dealer in coal.

To. Go to, go to; peace, peace! We must deal gently with him. Let me alone. How do you, Mal- 100 volio? How is't with you? What, man! defy the devil! Consider, he's an enemy to mankind.

Mal. Do you know what you say?

Mar. La you, an you speak ill of the devil, how he takes it at heart! Pray God he be not bewitched! 105

Fab. Carry his water to the wise woman.

Mar. Marry, and it shall be done tomorrow morn- ing if I live. My lady would not lose him for more than I'll say.

Mal. How now, mistress? 110

Mar. O Lord!

To. Prithee hold thy peace. This is not the way. Do you not see you move him? Let me alone with him.

Fab. No way but gentleness; gently, gently. The 115 fiend is rough and will not be roughly used.

To. Why, how now, my bawcock? How dost thou, chuck?

Mal. Sir!

To. Ay, biddy, come with me. What, man! 'tis not 120 for gravity to play at cherry-pit with Satan. Hang him, foul collier!

Mar. Get him to say his prayers. Good Sir Toby, get him to pray.

Mal. My prayers, minx? 125

Mar. No, I warrant you, he will not hear of godli- ness.

Mal. Go hang yourselves all! You are idle shallow

134. genius: innermost nature.

136-37. take air and taint: become known and thus be spoiled.

145. bar: bar of judgment.

147. May morning: i.e., antic season.

151. is't: it is.

155. admire: marvel.

things; I am not of your element. You shall know
more hereafter.   *Exit.* 130

To. Is't possible?

Fab. If this were played upon a stage now, I could
condemn it as an improbable fiction.

To. His very genius hath taken the infection of the
device, man.   135

Mar. Nay, pursue him now, lest the device take
air and taint.

Fab. Why, we shall make him mad indeed.

Mar. The house will be the quieter.

To. Come, we'll have him in a dark room and 140
bound. My niece is already in the belief that he's
mad. We may carry it thus, for our pleasure and his
penance, till our very pastime, tired out of breath,
prompt us to have mercy on him; at which time we
will bring the device to the bar and crown thee for a 145
finder of madmen. But see, but see!

Enter *Sir Andrew*.

Fab. More matter for a May morning.

And. Here's the challenge; read it. I warrant
there's vinegar and pepper in't.

Fab. Is't so saucy?   150

And. Ay, is't, I warrant him. Do but read.

To. Give me. [*Reads*] "Youth, whatsoever thou art,
thou art but a scurvy fellow."

Fab. Good, and valiant.

To. [*Reads*] "Wonder not nor admire not in thy 155

174. my hope is better: i.e., he hopes he will have no need of God's mercy because he will defeat Cesario.

180. commerce: communication.

183. bum-baily: bailiff.

mind why I do call thee so, for I will show thee no reason for't."

Fab. A good note! That keeps you from the blow of·the law.

To. [*Reads*] "Thou comest to the Lady Olivia, and 160 in my sight she uses thee kindly. But thou liest in thy throat; that is not the matter I challenge thee for."

Fab. Very brief, and to exceeding good sense— less.

To. [*Reads*] "I will waylay thee going home; 165 where if it be thy chance to kill me"—

Fab. Good.

To. [*Reads*] "Thou killst me like a rogue and a villain."

Fab. Still you keep o' the windy side of the law. 170 Good.

To. [*Reads*] "Fare thee well, and God have mercy upon one of our souls! He may have mercy upon mine, but my hope is better; and so look to thyself. Thy friend, as thou usest him, and thy sworn enemy, 175

"ANDREW AGUECHEEK."

If this letter move him not, his legs cannot. I'll give't him.

Mar. You may have very fit occasion for't. He is now in some commerce with my lady and will by- 180 and-by depart.

To. Go, Sir Andrew! Scout me for him at the cor-ner of the orchard like a bum-baily. So soon as ever thou seest him, draw; and as thou drawst, swear hor-rible; for it comes to pass oft that a terrible oath, 185 with a swaggering accent sharply twanged off, gives

187. **approbation:** affirmative evidence; **proof:** trial.

189. **let me alone:** i.e., no one can equal me.

196. **clodpoll:** blockhead.

202. **cockatrices:** fabulous creatures whose glances could kill.

203-4. **Give them way:** make room for them.

205. **horrid:** frightful. The word had much stronger meaning in Shakespeare's time than it does today.

208. **unchary:** generously.

A cockatrice
From Joachim Camerarius,
Symbolorum et emblematum centuriae tres (1605).

manhood more approbation than ever proof itself
would have earned him. Away!

And. Nay, let me alone for swearing.   *Exit.*

To. Now will not I deliver his letter; for the be- 190
havior of the young gentleman gives him out to be
of good capacity and breeding; his employment between his lord and my niece confirms no less. Therefore this letter, being so excellently ignorant, will
breed no terror in the youth. He will find it comes 195
from a clodpoll. But, sir, I will deliver his challenge
by word of mouth, set upon Aguecheek a notable
report of valor, and drive the gentleman (as I know
his youth will aptly receive it) into a most hideous
opinion of his rage, skill, fury, and impetuosity. This 200
will so fright them both that they will kill one another by the look, like cockatrices.

Enter *Olivia* and *Viola.*

Fab. Here he comes with your niece. Give them
way till he take leave, and presently after him.

To. I will meditate the while upon some horrid 205
message for a challenge.

[*Exeunt Sir Toby, Fabian, and Maria.*]

Oli. I have said too much unto a heart of stone
And laid mine honor too unchary out.
There's something in me that reproves my fault;
But such a headstrong potent fault it is   210
That it but mocks reproof.

Vio. With the same 'havior that your passion bears
Goes on my master's grief.

223. **acquit:** release.

225. **A fiend like thee might bear my soul to hell:** a devil as charming as you would be welcome to take me to hell.

230. **despite:** anger.

231-32. **Dismount thy tuck:** draw thy sword; **yare:** quick.

Oli. Here, wear this jewel for me; 'tis my picture.
Refuse it not; it hath no tongue to vex you.   215
And I beseech you come again tomorrow.
What shall you ask of me that I'll deny,
That honor, saved, may upon asking give?
  Vio. Nothing but this—your true love for my mas-
    ter.   220
  Oli. How with mine honor may I give him that
Which I have given to you?
  Vio.   I will acquit you.
  Oli. Well, come again tomorrow. Fare thee well.
A fiend like thee might bear my soul to hell. [*Exit.*] 225

Enter [*Sir*] *Toby* and *Fabian.*

  To. Gentleman, God save thee!
  Vio. And you, sir.
  To. That defense thou hast, betake thee to't. Of
what nature the wrongs are thou hast done him, I
know not; but thy intercepter, full of despite, bloody 230
as the hunter, attends thee at the orchard end. Dismount thy tuck, be yare in thy preparation; for thy
assailant is quick, skillful, and deadly.
  Vio. You mistake, sir. I am sure no man hath any
quarrel to me. My remembrance is very free and 235
clear from any image of offense done to any man.
  To. You'll find it otherwise, I assure you. Therefore, if you hold your life at any price, betake you
to your guard; for your opposite hath in him what
youth, strength, skill, and wrath can furnish man 240
withal.

243. knight, dubbed with unhatched rapier: a knight dubbed with an ornamental sword in the court, far from the field of battle.

244. on carpet consideration: for considerations other than military prowess—usually a fee. The phrase "carpet knight" was a derogatory term.

248. Hob, nob: a phrase meaning "have or have not" or "give or take." Sir Toby is trying to suggest that Sir Andrew is a desperate character who demands a fight to the finish.

252-53. put quarrels purposely on: deliberately provoke quarrels with; **Belike:** most likely.

254. quirk: whim.

256. competent: sufficient.

260. meddle: take part.

270. mortal arbitrament: fatal conclusion.

Vio. I pray you, sir, what is he?

To. He is knight, dubbed with unhatched rapier
and on carpet consideration; but he is a devil in private brawl. Souls and bodies hath he divorced three; 245
and his incensement at this moment is so implacable
that satisfaction can be none but by pangs of death
and sepulcher. "Hob, nob" is his word; "give't or
take't."

Vio. I will return again into the house and desire 250
some conduct of the lady. I am no fighter. I have
heard of some kind of men that put quarrels purposely on others to taste their valor. Belike this is a man
of that quirk.

To. Sir, no. His indignation derives itself out of a 255
very competent injury; therefore get you on and give
him his desire. Back you shall not to the house, unless you undertake that with me which with as much
safety you might answer him. Therefore on! or strip
your sword stark naked; for meddle you must, that's 260
certain, or forswear to wear iron about you.

Vio. This is as uncivil as strange. I beseech you do
me this courteous office, as to know of the knight
what my offense to him is. It is something of my negligence, nothing of my purpose. 265

To. I will do so. Signior Fabian, stay you by this
gentleman till my return. *Exit.*

Vio. Pray you, sir, do you know of this matter?

Fab. I know the knight is incensed against you,
even to a mortal arbitrament; but nothing of the cir- 270
cumstance more.

Vio. I beseech you, what manner of man is he?

284-85. virago: violent woman. Though Sir Toby uses the feminine term, he simply means a fire-eating devil; **rapier, scabbard, and all:** that is, he needed his scabbard as well as his rapier for defense; **stuck-in:** thrust.

286-87. mortal motion: fatal movement; **inevitable:** impossible to parry; **on the answer he pays you:** in parrying your thrust he jabs you in return.

296. motion: offer, i.e., Sir Andrew's horse to forget the whole thing.

297-98. perdition of souls: that is, death and damnation of one or both participants.

Fab. Nothing of that wonderful promise, to read
him by his form, as you are like to find him in the
proof of his valor. He is indeed, sir, the most skillful, 275
bloody, and fatal opposite that you could possibly
have found in any part of Illyria. Will you walk towards him? I will make your peace with him if I
can.

Vio. I shall be much bound to you for't. I am one 280
that had rather go with sir priest than sir knight. I
care not who knows so much of my mettle. *Exeunt.*

Enter [*Sir*] *Toby* and [*Sir*] *Andrew.*

To. Why, man, he's a very devil; I have not seen
such a virago. I had a pass with him, rapier, scabbard,
and all, and he gives me the stuck-in with such a 285
mortal motion that it is inevitable; and on the answer
he pays you as surely as your feet hit the ground they
step on. They say he has been fencer to the Sophy.

And. Pox on't, I'll not meddle with him.

To. Ay, but he will not now be pacified. Fabian 290
can scarce hold him yonder.

And. Plague on't, an I thought he had been valiant,
and so cunning in fence, I'd have seen him damned
ere I'd have challenged him. Let him let the matter
slip, and I'll give him my horse, grey Capilet.   295

To. I'll make the motion. Stand here; make a good
show on't. This shall end without the perdition of
souls. [*Aside*] Marry, I'll ride your horse as well as I
ride you.

300. **take up:** make up, resolve.

302. **He is as horribly conceited of him:** that is, Cesario has as terrifying a conception of Aguecheek.

305. **for's:** for his; **hath better bethought him:** has had second thoughts.

313. **bout:** pass.

314. **duello:** dueling code.

Enter *Fabian* and *Viola*.

I have his horse to take up the quarrel. I have per- 300
suaded him the youth's a devil.

Fab. He is as horribly conceited of him; and pants
and looks pale, as if a bear were at his heels.

To. There's no remedy, sir; he will fight with you
for's oath sake. Marry, he hath better bethought him 305
of his quarrel, and he finds that now scarce to be
worth talking of. Therefore draw for the supportance
of his vow. He protests he will not hurt you.

Vio. [*Aside*] Pray God defend me! A little thing
would make me tell them how much I lack of a man. 310

Fab. Give ground if you see him furious.

To. Come, Sir Andrew, there's no remedy. The
gentleman will for his honor's sake have one bout
with you; he cannot by the duello avoid it; but he
has promised me, as he is a gentleman and a soldier, 315
he will not hurt you. Come on, to't!

And. Pray God he keep his oath!   [*Draws.*]

Enter *Antonio*.

Vio. I do assure you 'tis against my will. [*Draws.*]

Ant. Put up your sword. If this young gentleman
Have done offense, I take the fault on me;   320
If you offend him, I for him defy you.

To. You, sir? Why, what are you?

Ant. [*Draws*] One, sir, that for his love dares yet
   do more

326. **undertaker:** surety, protection.

329. **anon:** at once.

332-33. **He will bear you easily:** Sir Andrew praises the virtues of his horse.

338. **favor:** features, see II. iv. 27.

T E R Z A
QVINTA GVARDIA STRETTA,
difensiua, perfetta; nata da meza punta sopra-
mano, offensiua, da cui nasce un mezo
rouescio tondo.

Fencing guard.
From Angelo Vizani, *Trattato dello schermo* (1588). 71

Than you have heard him brag to you he will.   325
   To. Nay, if you be an undertaker, I am for you.
                                    [*Draws.*]

Enter *Officers.*

   Fab. O good Sir Toby, hold! Here come the offi-
cers.
   To. I'll be with you anon.
   Vio. Pray, sir, put your sword up, if you please.   330
   And. Marry, will I, sir; and for that I promised
you, I'll be as good as my word. He will bear you
easily, and reins well.
   1. Off. This is the man; do thy office.
   2. Off. Antonio, I arrest thee at the suit   335
Of Count Orsino.
   Ant.   You do mistake me, sir.
   1. Off. No, sir, no jot. I know your favor well,
Though now you have no sea-cap on your head.
Take him away. He knows I know him well.   340
   Ant. I must obey. [*To Viola*] This comes with
      seeking you.
But there's no remedy; I shall answer it.
What will you do, now my necessity
Makes me to ask you for my purse? It grieves me   345
Much more for what I cannot do for you
Than what befalls myself. You stand amazed,
But be of comfort.
   2. Off. Come, sir, away.
   Ant. I must entreat of you some of that money.   350
   Vio. What money, sir?

356. **my present:** the money which I have about me.

357. **coffer:** funds.

359-60. **Is't possible that my deserts to you/ Can lack persuasion:** is it possible that my loyalty and merit cannot sway you.

361. **unsound:** unstable; i.e., unmanly.

377. **Most venerable worth:** worthiness of the highest respect; **did I devotion:** I paid homage.

380. **done good feature shame:** disgraced your fair appearance.

For the fair kindness you have showed me here,
And part being prompted by your present trouble,
Out of my lean and low ability
I'll lend you something. My having is not much.   355
I'll make division of my present with you.
Hold, there's half my coffer.

Ant.   Will you deny me now?
Is't possible that my deserts to you
Can lack persuasion? Do not tempt my misery,   360
Lest that it make me so unsound a man
As to upbraid you with those kindnesses
That I have done for you.

Vio.   I know of none,
Nor know I you by voice or any feature.   365
I hate ingratitude more in a man
Than lying, vainness, babbling drunkenness,
Or any taint of vice whose strong corruption
Inhabits our frail blood.

Ant.   O heavens themselves!   370

2. Off. Come, sir, I pray you go.

Ant. Let me speak a little. This youth that you see
        here
I snatched one half out of the jaws of death;
Relieved him with such sanctity of love,   375
And to his image, which methought did promise
Most venerable worth, did I devotion.

1. Off. What's that to us? The time goes by. Away!

Ant. But, O, how vile an idol proves this god!
Thou hast, Sebastian, done good feature shame.   380
In nature there's no blemish but the mind;
None can be called deformed but the unkind.

383. **beauteous evil:** beautiful but wicked person.

384. **empty trunks, o'erflourished by the devil:** hollow chests decorated by the Devil to delude the unwary.

388. **from such passion fly:** derive from such anger.

393. **saws:** wise sayings.

394-95. **I my brother know/ Yet living in my glass:** that is, Viola and her brother look so much alike that Viola seems to see him each time she looks in the mirror in her masculine dress.

397. **Still:** always; see II. v. 173.

398-99. **For him I imitate:** Viola means that she has dressed as she remembered her brother. Shakespeare inserts this explanation and the other reference to the resemblance between brother and sister to make the confusion of identities a little more credible; **if it prove,/ Tempests are kind, and salt waves fresh in love:** if it proves true that Sebastian is alive, I can believe that tempests are kind and the salt waves have been made fresh by love.

400. **paltry:** contemptible.

406. **'Slid:** by God's eyelid.

410. **event:** outcome; see II. iii. 176.

Virtue is beauty; but the beauteous evil
Are empty trunks, o'erflourished by the devil.

   1. Off. The man grows mad. Away with him! 385
     Come, come, sir.

   Ant. Lead me on.   *Exit [with Officers].*

   Vio. Methinks his words do from such passion fly
That he believes himself; so do not I.
Prove true, imagination, O, prove true,   390
That I, dear brother, be now ta'en for you!

   To. Come hither, knight; come hither, Fabian.
We'll whisper o'er a couplet or two of most sage saws.

   Vio. He named Sebastian. I my brother know
Yet living in my glass. Even such and so   395
In favor was my brother, and he went
Still in this fashion, color, ornament,
For him I imitate. O, if it prove,
Tempests are kind, and salt waves fresh in love!

                            [Exit.]

   To. A very dishonest paltry boy, and more a cow- 400
ard than a hare. His dishonesty appears in leaving his
friend here in necessity and denying him; and for his
cowardship, ask Fabian.

   Fab. A coward, a most devout coward; religious
in it.   405

   And. 'Slid, I'll after him again and beat him!

   To. Do; cuff him soundly, but never draw thy
sword.

   And. An I do not—   *[Exit.]*

   Fab. Come, let's see the event.   410

   To. I dare lay any money 'twill be nothing yet.

                            Exeunt.

TWELFTH NIGHT

ACT IV

IV. i. Feste, sent in quest of Cesario, finds Sebastian, who cannot comprehend his message. Sir Andrew, Sir Toby, and Fabian enter and Sir Andrew attacks Sebastian, who returns his blow with professional skill. Sir Toby, slightly befuddled, draws and joins the fray but Olivia intervenes and orders everyone away but Sebastian.

10. **vent:** express.

14-5. **I am afraid this great lubber, the world, will prove a cockney:** I fear this awkward and stupid lout, the world, will prove to be a moron. **Cockney** in Elizabethan English had varied meanings but it was commonly used for milksop and stupid fellow.

15-6. **ungird thy strangeness:** cast off your pretense of being a stranger.

18. **Greek:** Sebastian does not understand the Clown's language any more than if he spoke Greek.

ACT IV

Scene I. [Before Olivia's house.]

Enter *Sebastian* and *Clown*.

Clown. Will you make me believe that I am not
sent for you?

Seb. Go to, go to, thou art a foolish fellow. Let me
be clear of thee.

Clown. Well held out, i' faith! No, I do not know 5
you; nor I am not sent to you by my lady, to bid you
come speak with her; nor your name is not Master
Cesario; nor this is not my nose neither. Nothing
that is so is so.

Seb. I prithee vent thy folly somewhere else. Thou 10
knowst not me.

Clown. Vent my folly! He has heard that word of
some great man, and now applies it to a fool. Vent
my folly! I am afraid this great lubber, the world,
will prove a cockney. I prithee now, ungird thy 15
strangeness, and tell me what I shall vent to my lady.
Shall I vent to her that thou art coming?

Seb. I prithee, foolish Greek, depart from me.
There's money for thee. If you tarry longer,
I shall give worse payment. 20

74

23. **after fourteen years' purchase:** this phrase derives from land tenure and implies here a very long time before wise men would get a good report from the fools.

30. **straight:** immediately.

35. **stroke:** struck.

39. **You are well fleshed:** you have had an ample taste of blood.

45. **malapert:** impudent.

Clown. By my troth, thou hast an open hand.
These wise men that give fools money get themselves a good report—after fourteen years' purchase.

Enter [*Sir*] *Andrew*, [*Sir*] *Toby*, and *Fabian.*

And. Now, sir, have I met you again? There's for
you!　　　　　　　　　　　　[*Striking Sebastian.*]　25
Seb. Why, there's for thee, and there, and there!
　　　　　　　　　　　　　　[*Returning the blow.*]
Are all the people mad?
To. Hold, sir, or I'll throw your dagger o'er the
house.
Clown. This will I tell my lady straight. I would　30
not be in some of your coats for twopence.　[*Exit.*]
To. Come on, sir; hold!
And. Nay, let him alone. I'll go another way to
work with him. I'll have an action of battery against
him, if there be any law in Illyria. Though I stroke　35
him first, yet it's no matter for that.
Seb. Let go thy hand.
To. Come, sir, I will not let you go. Come, my
young soldier, put up your iron. You are well fleshed.
Come on.　　　　　　　　　　　　　　　　　　　40
Seb. I will be free from thee. What wouldst thou
　now?
If thou darest tempt me further, draw thy sword.
To. What, what? Nay then, I must have an ounce
or two of this malapert blood from you.　[*Draws.*]　45

48. **ungracious:** lacking in grace, rude.

53. **Rudesby:** barbarian.

56. **extent:** demonstration.

61. **Beshrew:** curse; see II. iii. 80.

62. **started one poor heart of mine, in thee:**
Olivia, in love with Cesario, is saying that Sir Toby,
by drawing his sword against him, had stirred her
heart. Shakespeare is playing on the word "heart"
and is using a hunting term, **start,** which means to
flush from a covert.

63. **What relish is in this:** what am I to make of
this.

64. **Or:** either.

65. **Lethe:** the river in Hades whose waters caused
forgetfulness.

Enter Olivia.

Oli. Hold, Toby! On thy life I charge thee hold!

To. Madam!

Oli. Will it be ever thus? Ungracious wretch,

Fit for the mountains and the barbarous caves,

Where manners ne'er were preached! Out of my   50
    sight!

Be not offended, dear Cesario.

Rudesby, be gone!

    [Exeunt Sir Toby, Sir Andrew, and Fabian.]
          I prithee, gentle friend,

Let thy fair wisdom, not thy passion, sway   55

In this uncivil and unjust extent

Against thy peace. Go with me to my house,

And hear thou there how many fruitless pranks

This ruffian hath botched up, that thou thereby

Mayst smile at this. Thou shalt not choose but go;   60

Do not deny. Beshrew his soul for me!

He started one poor heart of mine, in thee.

  Seb. What relish is in this? How runs the stream?

Or I am mad, or else this is a dream.

Let fancy still my sense in Lethe steep;   65

If it be thus to dream, still let me sleep!

  Oli. Nay, come, I prithee. Would thou'dst be ruled
    by me!

  Seb. Madam, I will.

  Oli.   O, say so, and so be!   70

                Exeunt.

IV. ii. Feste, disguised as the curate Sir Topas, torments Malvolio, whom they have locked up in a dark place. The Clown plays his part with glee, but Sir Toby, already in disgrace with his niece, would gladly be out of the plot.

⚊⚊⚊⚊⚊⚊⚊⚊

4. **dissemble:** disguise.

10. **competitors:** colleagues in this enterprise.

13-5. **Bonos dies:** good day; **old hermit of Prague . . . King Gorboduc:** the Clown is talking pseudo-learned nonsense to sound impressive in the manner of a cleric.

Scene II. [Olivia's house.]

Enter *Maria* and *Clown*.

Mar. Nay, I prithee put on this gown and this
beard; make him believe thou art Sir Topas the curate;
do it quickly. I'll call Sir Toby the whilst.   [*Exit.*]

Clown. Well, I'll put it on, and I will dissemble
myself in't, and I would I were the first that ever   5
dissembled in such a gown. I am not tall enough to
become the function well, nor lean enough to be
thought a good student; but to be said an honest
man and a good housekeeper goes as fairly as to say
a careful man and a great scholar. The competitors   10
enter.

Enter [*Sir*] *Toby* [and *Maria*].

To. Jove bless thee, Master Parson.
Clown. *Bonos dies,* Sir Toby; for, as the old hermit
of Prague, that never saw pen and ink, very wittily
said to a niece of King Gorboduc, "That that is is";   15
so I, being Master Parson, am Master Parson; for
what is "that" but "that," and "is" but "is"?
To. To him, Sir Topas.
Clown. What ho, I say. Peace in this prison!
To. The knave counterfeits well; a good knave.   20

Malvolio within.

Mal. Who calls there?
Clown. Sir Topas the curate, who comes to visit
Malvolio the lunatic.

26. hyperbolical: exaggerated, a rhetorical term. Feste means that the demon supposedly possessing Malvolio is violent.

38. barricadoes: barricades; **clerestories:** upper windows. The Clown uses words with no logical meaning but designed as nonsense.

49-50. constant question: rational line of talk.

51. Pythagoras: a Greek philosopher, to whom the doctrine of the transmigration of souls was attributed.

53. happily: by chance.

Pythagoras.

From Guillaume Rouille, *Del prontuario de le medaglie de piu illustri, & fulgenti huomini & donne* (1553).

Mal. Sir Topas, Sir Topas, good Sir Topas, go to
my lady.   25

Clown. Out, hyperbolical fiend! How vexest thou
this man! Talkest thou nothing but of ladies?

To. Well said, Master Parson.

Mal. Sir Topas, never was man thus wronged.
Good Sir Topas, do not think I am mad. They have   30
laid me here in hideous darkness.

Clown. Fie, thou dishonest Satan! I call thee by
the most modest terms; for I am one of those gentle
ones that will use the Devil himself with courtesy.
Sayst thou that house is dark?   35

Mal. As hell, Sir Topas.

Clown. Why, it hath bay windows transparent as
barricadoes, and the clerestories toward the south
north are as lustrous as ebony; and yet complainest
thou of obstruction?   40

Mal. I am not mad, Sir Topas. I say to you this
house is dark.

Clown. Madman, thou errest. I say there is no
darkness but ignorance, in which thou art more puzzled than the Egyptians in their fog.   45

Mal. I say this house is as dark as ignorance,
though ignorance were as dark as hell; and I say
there was never man thus abused. I am no more
mad than you are. Make the trial of it in any constant
question.   50

Clown. What is the opinion of Pythagoras concerning wild fowl?

Mal. That the soul of our grandam might happily
inhabit a bird.

60. **allow of thy wits:** admit that you have your wits about you.

65. **Nay, I am for all waters:** indeed, I can do anything. The precise meaning of this figure of speech is lost.

70. **delivered:** freed.

78. **perdie:** a corruption of *par dieu*, but having no more force than "indeed."

Clown. What thinkst thou of his opinion?   55

Mal. I think nobly of the soul and no way approve
his opinion.

Clown. Fare thee well. Remain thou still in darkness. Thou shalt hold the opinion of Pythagoras ere
I will allow of thy wits, and fear to kill a woodcock,   60
lest thou dispossess the soul of thy grandam. Fare
thee well.

Mal. Sir Topas, Sir Topas!

To. My most exquisite Sir Topas!

Clown. Nay, I am for all waters.   65

Mar. Thou mightst have done this without thy
beard and gown. He sees thee not.

To. To him in thine own voice, and bring me word
how thou findst him. I would we were well rid of
this knavery. If he may be conveniently delivered,   70
I would he were; for I am now so far in offense with
my niece that I cannot pursue with any safety this
sport to the upshot. Come by-and-by to my cham-
ber.   *Exit [with Maria].*

Clown. [*Singing*] "Hey, Robin, jolly Robin,   75
                        Tell me how thy lady does."

Mal. Fool!

Clown. "My lady is unkind, perdie!"

Mal. Fool!

Clown. "Alas, why is she so?"   80

Mal. Fool, I say!

Clown. "She loves another"—Who calls, ha?

Mal. Good fool, as ever thou wilt deserve well at
my hand, help me to a candle, and pen, ink, and pa-

89-90. how fell you besides your five wits:
how came you to lose your senses.

93. But: only.

95. propertied: made a mere tool of.

98. Advise you: consider carefully.

108. shent: disgraced.

per. As I am a gentleman, I will live to be thankful 85
to thee for't.

Clown. Master Malvolio?

Mal. Ay, good fool.

Clown. Alas, sir, how fell you besides your five
wits?   90

Mal. Fool, there was never man so notoriously
abused. I am as well in my wits, fool, as thou art.

Clown. But as well? Then you are mad indeed,
if you be no better in your wits than a fool.

Mal. They have here propertied me; keep me in 95
darkness, send ministers to me, asses, and do all they
can to face me out of my wits.

Clown. Advise you what you say. The minister is
here.—Malvolio, Malvolio, thy wits the heavens restore! Endeavor thyself to sleep and leave thy vain 100
bibble babble.

Mal. Sir Topas!

Clown. Maintain no words with him, good fellow.—Who, I, sir? Not I, sir. God be wi' you, good
Sir Topas!—Marry, amen.—I will, sir, I will.   105

Mal. Fool, fool, fool, I say!

Clown. Alas, sir, be patient. What say you, sir? I
am shent for speaking to you.

Mal. Good fool, help me to some light and some
paper. I tell thee, I am as well in my wits as any man 110
in Illyria.

Clown. Well-a-day that you were, sir!

Mal. By this hand, I am. Good fool, some ink, paper, and light; and convey what I will set down to

128. the old Vice: a comic figure in the old morality plays.

IV. iii. Olivia has offered herself to Sebastian if he will consent to marry her at once. The situation is hard for Sebastian to understand but Olivia's beauty and her obvious position persuade him to accept.

my lady. It shall advantage thee more than ever the 115
bearing of letter did.

Clown. I will help you to't. But tell me true, are
you not mad indeed? or do you but counterfeit?

Mal. Believe me, I am not. I tell thee true.

Clown. Nay, I'll ne'er believe a madman till I see 120
his brains. I will fetch you light and paper and ink.

Mal. Fool, I'll requite it in the highest degree. I
prithee be gone.

Clown. [*Singing*]

       I am gone, sir;
       And anon, sir,   125
   I'll be with you again,
      In a trice,
      Like to the old Vice,
   Your need to sustain;
   Who, with dagger of lath,   130
   In his rage and his wrath,
      Cries "aha!" to the Devil.
   Like a mad lad,
   "Pare thy nails, dad."
      Adieu, goodman Devil.   135

                                    Exit.

Scene III. [Olivia's garden.]

Enter *Sebastian.*

Seb. This is the air; that is the glorious sun;
This pearl she gave me, I do feel't and see't;

6. **credit:** belief.

12. **instance:** precedent; **discourse:** rationality.

17. **sway:** rule; see II. iv. 38.

19. **Take and give back affairs and their dispatch:** listen to reports, make decisions, and see that business is attended to.

22. **deceivable:** deceiving, deceptive.

26. **chantry by:** nearby chapel.

29. **jealous:** skeptical.

And though 'tis wonder that enwraps me thus,
Yet 'tis not madness. Where's Antonio then?
I could not find him at the Elephant; 5
Yet there he was; and there I found this credit,
That he did range the town to seek me out.
His counsel now might do me golden service;
For though my soul disputes well with my sense
That this may be some error, but no madness, 10
Yet doth this accident and flood of fortune
So far exceed all instance, all discourse,
That I am ready to distrust mine eyes
And wrangle with my reason, that persuades me
To any other trust but that I am mad, 15
Or else the lady's mad. Yet, if 'twere so,
She could not sway her house, command her fol-
    lowers,
Take and give back affairs and their dispatch
With such a smooth, discreet, and stable bearing 20
As I perceive she does. There's something in't
That is deceivable. But here the lady comes.

Enter *Olivia* and *Priest*.

Oli. Blame not this haste of mine. If you mean
    well,
Now go with me and with this holy man 25
Into the chantry by. There, before him,
And underneath that consecrated roof,
Plight me the full assurance of your faith,
That my most jealous and too doubtful soul
May live at peace. He shall conceal it 30

31. **Whiles:** until.
32. **What time:** at which time.
33. **birth:** rank.
38. **That they may fairly note:** to indicate approval of.

Whiles you are willing it shall come to note,
What time we will our celebration keep
According to my birth. What do you say?

   Seb. I'll follow this good man and go with you
And having sworn truth, ever will be true.   35

   Oli. Then lead the way, good father; and heavens
      so shine
That they may fairly note this act of mine!

                                        Exeunt.

TWELFTH NIGHT

❧

ACT V

V. i. Antonio is brought before the Duke and creates some confusion by relating his adventures with Viola-Cesario, who he still thinks is Sebastian. Olivia adds to the confusion by entering and claiming Viola-Cesario as her husband, to Orsino's extreme dismay and displeasure. Sir Andrew and Sir Toby in the meantime have had another encounter with Sebastian; they enter wounded and blame their hurts upon Viola-Cesario. Everything is finally made clear when Sebastian himself appears and the company see Viola and Sebastian, twins, dressed alike, side by side. Viola promises to assume her maiden attire to prove her identity as Sebastian's sister. Orsino, remembering Viola's many expressions of affection, is content to abandon his hopeless love for Olivia and marry her.

Feste, persuaded by Malvolio to deliver a letter to Olivia about his wrongs, proceeds to read it. Olivia orders Malvolio's release. When he is brought into her presence, she admits that he has been badly treated but denies knowledge of the plot. The embittered Malvolio leaves, swearing vengeance upon them all. Fabian tells the whole story and discloses that Sir Toby has married Maria as a reward for her brilliant plot. A merry song by Feste brings the action to a close.

ACT V

Scene I. [Before Olivia's house.]

Enter *Clown* and *Fabian*.

Fab. Now as thou lovest me, let me see his letter.

Clown. Good Master Fabian, grant me another request.

Fab. Anything.

Clown. Do not desire to see this letter.   5

Fab. This is to give a dog, and in recompense desire my dog again.

Enter *Duke*, *Viola*, *Curio*, and *Lords*.

Duke. Belong you to the Lady Olivia, friends?

Clown. Ay, sir, we are some of her trappings.

Duke. I know thee well. How dost thou, my good   10
fellow?

Clown. Truly, sir, the better for my foes, and the worse for my friends.

Duke. Just the contrary: the better for thy friends.

Clown. No, sir, the worse.   15

Duke. How can that be?

Clown. Marry, sir, they praise me and make an ass

84

20. **abused**: deceived; see III. i. 118.

31. **ill counsel**: in urging me to **double-dealing**.

32. **your grace**: your virtue, with a pun on the designation "Your Grace" to which the Duke is entitled.

33. **it**: the ill counsel.

37. **triplex**: triple time.

40-1. **at this throw**: the Duke follows the Clown's humor in speaking as though they were playing dice.

of me. Now my foes tell me plainly I am an ass; so
that by my foes, sir, I profit in the knowledge of myself, and by my friends I am abused; so that, conclu- 20
sions to be as kisses, if your four negatives make your
two affirmatives, why then, the worse for my friends
and the better for my foes.

Duke. Why, this is excellent.

Clown. By my troth, sir, no; though it please you 25
to be one of my friends.

Duke. Thou shalt not be the worse for me. There's
gold.

Clown. But that it would be double-dealing, sir, I
would you could make it another. 30

Duke. O, you give me ill counsel.

Clown. Put your grace in your pocket, sir, for this
once, and let your flesh and blood obey it.

Duke. Well, I will be so much a sinner to be a
double-dealer. There's another. 35

Clown. Primo, secundo, tertio is a good play; and
the old saying is "The third pays for all." The triplex,
sir, is a good tripping measure; or the bells of Saint
Bennet, sir, may put you in mind—one, two, three.

Duke. You can fool no more money out of me at 40
this throw. If you will let your lady know I am here
to speak with her, and bring her along with you, it
may awake my bounty further.

Clown. Marry, sir, lullaby to your bounty till I
come again! I go, sir; but I would not have you to 45
think that my desire of having is the sin of covetous-
ness. But, as you say, sir, let your bounty take a nap;
I will awake it anon.   *Exit.*

52. **Vulcan:** the Roman god of war and metal-working, usually pictured as a smith.

53. **baubling:** trifling.

54. **For shallow draught and bulk unprizable:** valueless because of its small size and draught.

55. **scathful:** harmful.

56. **bottom:** vessel.

57. **very envy and the tongue of loss:** even his enemies who had suffered from his actions.

60. **fraught:** cargo; **Candy:** Candia, now known as Crete.

63. **desperate of shame and state:** reckless of disgrace and unmindful of his situation as an enemy in Orsino's dukedom.

64. **private brabble:** personal brawl.

66. **put strange speech upon me:** spoke to me strangely.

75. **on base and ground enough:** for sufficient reason.

Enter *Antonio* and *Officers*.

Vio. Here comes the man, sir, that did rescue me.
Duke. That face of his I do remember well;　　50
Yet when I saw it last, it was besmeared
As black as Vulcan in the smoke of war.
A baubling vessel was he captain of,
For shallow draught and bulk unprizable,
With which such scathful grapple did he make　　55
With the most noble bottom of our fleet
That very envy and the tongue of loss
Cried fame and honor on him. What's the matter?
1. Off. Orsino, this is that Antonio
That took the "Phœnix" and her fraught from Candy;　60
And this is he that did the "Tiger" board
When your young nephew Titus lost his leg.
Here in the streets, desperate of shame and state,
In private brabble did we apprehend him.
Vio. He did me kindness, sir; drew on my side;　　65
But in conclusion put strange speech upon me.
I know not what 'twas but distraction.
Duke. Notable pirate, thou salt-water thief!
What foolish boldness brought thee to their mercies
Whom thou in terms so bloody and so dear　　70
Hast made thine enemies?
Ant. 　　　　　　Orsino, noble sir,
Be pleased that I shake off these names you give me.
Antonio never yet was thief or pirate,
Though I confess, on base and ground enough,　　75

79. **wrack:** ruin.

83. **pure:** purely.

84. **adverse:** enemy.

88. **face me out of his acquaintance:** pretend that he did not know me.

91. **recommended to:** offered for.

96. **No int'rim:** without interruption.

Vulcan at his forge.

From Jean Baudoin, *Recueil d'emblemes divers* (1638–1639).

(See V. i. 52.)

Orsino's enemy. A witchcraft drew me hither.
That most ingrateful boy there by your side
From the rude sea's enraged and foamy mouth
Did I redeem. A wrack past hope he was.
His life I gave him, and did thereto add   80
My love without retention or restraint,
All his in dedication. For his sake
Did I expose myself (pure for his love)
Into the danger of this adverse town;
Drew to defend him when he was beset;   85
Where being apprehended, his false cunning
(Not meaning to partake with me in danger)
Taught him to face me out of his acquaintance,
And grew a twenty years removed thing
While one would wink; denied me mine own purse,   90
Which I had recommended to his use
Not half an hour before.
    Vio.   How can this be?
    Duke. When came he to this town?
    Ant. Today, my lord; and for three months before,   95
No int'rim, not a minute's vacancy,
Both day and night did we keep company.

Enter *Olivia* and *Attendants.*

    Duke. Here comes the Countess; now heaven
        walks on earth.
But for thee, fellow—fellow, thy words are madness.   100
Three months this youth hath tended upon me;
But more of that anon. Take him aside.

103-4. **What would my lord, but that he may not have:** what do you wish, except my love which you cannot have.

112. **fat and fulsome:** sickening.

117. **ingrate:** ungrateful; **unauspicious:** unfavorable.

119. **tendered:** offered.

120-21. **Even what it please my lord, that shall become him:** only whatever pleases you and is fitting for you.

123. **the Egyptian thief at point of death:** a character in Heliodorus' story of Theagenes and Chariclea, who tried to kill the woman he loved rather than lose her when threatened with capture.

125. **savors nobly:** smacks of nobility.

126. **to non-regardance cast my faith:** throw my devotion into the discard.

127. **instrument:** the youth with whom she has fallen in love.

128. **screws:** detaches.

130. **minion:** pet.

131. **tender:** hold.

132. **that cruel eye:** Olivia's esteem.

Oli. What would my lord, but that he may not
    have,
Wherein Olivia may seem serviceable?   105
Cesario, you do not keep promise with me.

Vio. Madam!

Duke. Gracious Olivia—

Oli. What do you say, Cesario?—Good my lord—

Vio. My lord would speak; my duty hushes me.   110

Oli. If it be aught to the old tune, my lord,
It is as fat and fulsome to mine ear
As howling after music.

Duke.   Still so cruel?

Oli. Still so constant, lord.   115

Duke. What, to perverseness? You uncivil lady,
To whose ingrate and unauspicious altars
My soul the faithful'st off'rings hath breathed out
That e'er devotion tendered! What shall I do?

Oli. Even what it please my lord, that shall be-   120
    come him.

Duke. Why should I not, had I the heart to do it,
Like to the Egyptian thief at point of death,
Kill what I love?—a savage jealousy
That sometime savors nobly. But hear me this: 125
Since you to non-regardance cast my faith,
And that I partly know the instrument
That screws me from my true place in your favor,
Live you the marble-breasted tyrant still.
But this your minion, whom I know you love,   130
And whom, by heaven I swear, I tender dearly,
Him will I tear out of that cruel eye

133. **in his master's spite:** in spite of his master's previously declared love for Olivia.

134-35. **ripe in mischief:** ready for trouble.

138. **jocund:** cheerfully.

139. **do you rest:** give you ease.

144-45. **If I do feign, you witnesses above/ Punish my life for tainting of my love:** if I swear falsely, the angels above punish me for besmirching my love.

146. **Ay me detested:** alas for me, despised; **beguiled:** deluded.

155. **sirrah:** a term of address expressing contempt or the assumption of authority on the part of the speaker.

158. **strangle thy propriety:** smother your identity.

159. **take thy fortunes up:** assume the good fortune that has come to you.

160. **that thou knowst thou art:** Olivia's husband.

161. **that thou fearest:** Orsino.

Where he sits crowned in his master's spite.

Come, boy, with me. My thoughts are ripe in mischief.   135

I'll sacrifice the lamb that I do love

To spite a raven's heart within a dove.

    Vio. And I, most jocund, apt, and willingly,

To do you rest a thousand deaths would die.

    Oli. Where goes Cesario?   140

    Vio.   After him I love

More than I love these eyes, more than my life,

More, by all mores, than e'er I shall love wife.

If I do feign, you witnesses above

Punish my life for tainting of my love!   145

    Oli. Ay me detested! how am I beguiled!

    Vio. Who does beguile you? Who does do you
wrong?

    Oli. Hast thou forgot thyself? Is it so long?

Call forth the holy father.   150

                     [Exit an Attendant.]

    Duke.   *[To Viola]* Come, away!

    Oli. Whither, my lord? Cesario, husband, stay.

    Duke. Husband?

    Oli.   Ay, husband. Can he that deny?

    Duke. Her husband, sirrah?   155

    Vio.   No, my lord, not I.

    Oli. Alas, it is the baseness of thy fear

That makes thee strangle thy propriety.

Fear not, Cesario; take thy fortunes up;

Be that thou knowst thou art, and then thou art   160

As great as that thou fearest.

163. **by thy reverence:** by the deep respect you command.

170. **holy close of lips:** nuptial kiss.

173. **Sealed in my function:** confirmed by my office of priest.

177. **sowed a grizzle on thy case:** turned your hair grey. **Grizzle** is a term for mingled dark and grey hair.

178. **craft:** trickery.

179. **trip:** that is, attempt to trip someone else. The sense of this passage is that the youth will so overreach himself in his trickery that he will trip up and thus encompass his own downfall.

184. **Hold little faith:** at least retain some little portion of faith.

Enter Priest.

O, welcome, father!
Father, I charge thee by thy reverence
Here to unfold—though lately we intended
To keep in darkness what occasion now   165
Reveals before 'tis ripe—what thou dost know
Hath newly passed between this youth and me.
  Priest. A contract of eternal bond of love,
Confirmed by mutual joinder of your hands,
Attested by the holy close of lips,   170
Strengthened by interchangement of your rings;
And all the ceremony of this compact
Sealed in my function, by my testimony;
Since when, my watch hath told me, toward my grave
I have traveled but two hours.   175
  Duke. O thou dissembling cub! What wilt thou be
When time hath sowed a grizzle on thy case?
Or will not else thy craft so quickly grow
That thine own trip shall be thine overthrow?
Farewell, and take her; but direct thy feet   180
Where thou and I, henceforth, may never meet.
  Vio. My lord, I do protest—
  Oli.   O, do not swear!
Hold little faith, though thou hast too much fear.

Enter Sir Andrew.

  And. For the love of God, a surgeon! Send one   185
presently to Sir Toby.
  Oli. What's the matter?
  And. Has broke my head across, and has given Sir

189. **coxcomb:** head.

194. **incardinate:** incarnate.

196. **Od's lifelings:** by God's life.

203. **set nothing by:** think nothing of.

204. **halting:** limping.

206. **othergates:** otherwise.

209. **Sot:** fool; see I. v. 124.

211. **set:** glassy from drink.

212. **passy measures pavin:** This phrase may simply be drunken nonsense but scholars have attempted to see in it an allusion to a slow dance, since there is an Italian phrase "passamezzo," meaning a slow measure, and a pavan is also a slow dance. The relevance of this to the surgeon is elusive.

214. **havoc:** devastation.

Toby a bloody coxcomb too. For the love of God,
your help! I had rather than forty pound I were at   190
home.

Oli. Who has done this, Sir Andrew?

And. The Count's gentleman, one Cesario. We took
him for a coward, but he's the very Devil incardinate.

Duke. My gentleman Cesario?   195

And. Od's lifelings, here he is! You broke my head
for nothing; and that that I did, I was set on to do't
by Sir Toby.

Vio. Why do you speak to me? I never hurt you.
You drew your sword upon me without cause,   200
But I bespake you fair and hurt you not.

Enter [*Sir*] *Toby* and *Clown.*

And. If a bloody coxcomb be a hurt, you have hurt
me. I think you set nothing by a bloody coxcomb.
Here comes Sir Toby halting—you shall hear more.
But if he had not been in drink, he would have   205
tickled you othergates than he did.

Duke. How now, gentleman? How is't with you?

To. That's all one! Has hurt me, and there's the
end on't.—Sot, didst see Dick Surgeon, sot?

Clown. O, he's drunk, Sir Toby, an hour agone. His   210
eyes were set at eight i' the morning.

To. Then he's a rogue and a passy measures pavin.
I hate a drunken rogue.

Oli. Away with him! Who hath made this havoc
with them?

215

217. dressed: treated by the surgeon.

224. throw a strange regard upon me: look at me strangely.

228. habit: costume; see II. v. 165 and III. iv. 77.

230. a natural perspective: an illusion created by nature itself.

241-42. that deity in my nature/ Of here and everywhere: the ability of God to be everywhere at once.

And. I'll help you, Sir Toby, because we'll be
dressed together.

To. Will you help—an ass-head and a coxcomb
and a knave—a thin-faced knave, a gull?

Oli. Get him to bed, and let his hurt be looked to. 220
[*Exeunt Sir Toby, Sir Andrew, Clown, and Fabian.*]

Enter *Sebastian.*

Seb. I am sorry, madam, I have hurt your kinsman;
But had it been the brother of my blood,
I must have done no less with wit and safety.
You throw a strange regard upon me, and by that
I do perceive it hath offended you.   225
Pardon me, sweet one, even for the vows
We made each other but so late ago.

Duke. One face, one voice, one habit, and two persons!

A natural perspective, that is and is not!   230

Seb. Antonio! O my dear Antonio!
How have the hours racked and tortured me
Since I have lost thee!

Ant. Sebastian are you?

Seb.　　　　　　　　　　Fearst thou that, Antonio? 235

Ant. How have you made division of yourself?
An apple cleft in two is not more twin
Than these two creatures. Which is Sebastian?

Oli. Most wonderful!

Seb. Do I stand there? I never had a brother;   240
Nor can there be that deity in my nature
Of here and everywhere. I had a sister,

244. **Of charity:** out of goodness, tell me.

248. **suited:** dressed.

252-53. **in that dimension grossly clad/ Which from the womb I did participate:** in that physical body which I have possessed since birth.

254. **as the rest goes even:** as the evidence seems to indicate.

264. **lets:** hinders.

265. **masculine usurped attire:** improperly assumed male dress.

267. **cohere and jump:** agree, prove conclusively.

270. **maiden weeds:** woman's clothing.

Whom the blind waves and surges have devoured.
Of charity, what kin are you to me?
What countryman? what name? what parentage?   245
    Vio. Of Messaline; Sebastian was my father—
Such a Sebastian was my brother too;
So went he suited to his watery tomb.
If spirits can assume both form and suit,
You come to fright us.   250
    Seb.   A spirit I am indeed,
But am in that dimension grossly clad
Which from the womb I did participate.
Were you a woman, as the rest goes even,
I should my tears let fall upon your cheek   255
And say, "Thrice welcome, drowned Viola!"
    Vio. My father had a mole upon his brow—
    Seb. And so had mine.
    Vio. And died that day when Viola from her birth
Had numbered thirteen years.   260
    Seb. O, that record is lively in my soul!
He finished indeed his mortal act
That day that made my sister thirteen years.
    Vio. If nothing lets to make us happy both
But this my masculine usurped attire,   265
Do not embrace me till each circumstance
Of place, time, fortune do cohere and jump
That I am Viola; which to confirm,
I'll bring you to a captain in this town,
Where lie my maiden weeds; by whose gentle help   270
I was preserved to serve this noble Count.
All the occurrence of my fortune since
Hath been between this lady and this lord.

276. **nature to her bias drew in that:** a bowling term; i.e., you followed a natural inclination thereby.

280. **amazed:** dumbstruck.

281. **as yet the glass seems true:** a further reference to a perspective glass, a gadget which presented distorted images. The Duke means that in this case the glass seems to be presenting a true picture.

288. **orbed continent:** the sun.

293. **upon some action:** as the result of some legal action.

294. **in durance:** jailed.

296. **enlarge:** free.

299. **extracting:** distracting.

Seb. [*To Olivia*] So comes it, lady, you have been
    mistook. 275
But nature to her bias drew in that.
You would have been contracted to a maid;
Nor are you therein, by my life, deceived:
You are betrothed both to a maid and man.

Duke. Be not amazed; right noble is his blood. 280
If this be so, as yet the glass seems true,
I shall have share in this most happy wrack.
[*To Viola*] Boy, thou hast said to me a thousand
    times
Thou never shouldst love woman like to me. 285

Vio. And all those sayings will I over swear,
And all those swearings keep as true in soul
As doth that orbed continent the fire
That severs day from night.

Duke.   Give me thy hand, 290
And let me see thee in thy woman's weeds.

Vio. The captain that did bring me first on shore
Hath my maid's garments. He upon some action
Is now in durance, at Malvolio's suit,
A gentleman, and follower of my lady's. 295

Oli. He shall enlarge him. Fetch Malvolio hither.
And yet alas! now I remember me,
They say, poor gentleman, he's much distract.

       Enter *Clown* with a letter, and *Fabian*.

A most extracting frenzy of mine own
From my remembrance clearly banished his. 300
How does he, sirrah?

302. **Belzebub:** prince of the devils.

306. **skills not much:** matters little.

310. **delivers:** presents the message of.

315. **vox:** voice. The Clown has begun to read Malvolio's letter in an exaggerated tone which he thinks is suitable to a madman's message.

318. **perpend:** consider carefully.

A noble Englishwoman.

From Pietro Bertelli, *Diversarum nationum habitus* (1594).

Clown. Truly, madam, he holds Belzebub at the
stave's end as well as a man in his case may do. Has
here writ a letter to you; I should have given't you
today morning. [*Offers the letter.*] But as a madman's 305
epistles are no gospels, so it skills not much when
they are delivered.

Oli. Open't and read it.

Clown. Look then to be well edified, when the fool
delivers the madman. [*Reads loudly*] "By the Lord, 310
madam"—

Oli. How now? Art thou mad?

Clown. No, madam, I do but read madness. An
your ladyship will have it as it ought to be, you must
allow vox. 315

Oli. Prithee read i' thy right wits.

Clown. So I do, madonna; but to read his right
wits is to read thus. Therefore perpend, my princess,
and give ear.

Oli. [*To Fabian*] Read it you, sirrah. 320

Fab. (*Reads*) "By the Lord, madam, you wrong
me, and the world shall know it. Though you have
put me into darkness, and given your drunken cousin
rule over me, yet have I the benefit of my senses as
well as your ladyship. I have your own letter that in- 325
duced me to the semblance I put on; with the which
I doubt not but to do myself much right, or you much
shame. Think of me as you please. I leave my duty a
little unthought of, and speak out of my injury.

　　　　　"THE MADLY USED MALVOLIO." 330

Oli. Did he write this?

334. **delivered:** freed.

335-39. **so please you, these things further thought on,/ To think me as well a sister as a wife,/ One day shall crown the alliance on't . . ./ Here at my house and at my proper cost:** if you are willing, after due consideration, to think of me as a sister-in-law instead of a wife, the same day we shall complete the ceremonies at my house and at my personal expense.

340. **apt:** eager.

341. **quits:** discharges.

Clown. Ay, madam.

Duke. This savors not much of distraction.

Oli. See him delivered, Fabian; bring him hither.

[*Exit Fabian.*]

My lord, so please you, these things further thought 335
    on,

To think me as well a sister as a wife,

One day shall crown the alliance on't, so please you,

Here at my house and at my proper cost.

  Duke. Madam, I am most apt t' embrace your offer. 340
[*To Viola*] Your master quits you; and for your serv-
    ice done him,

So much against the mettle of your sex,

So far beneath your soft and tender breeding,

And since you called me master, for so long,   345

Here is my hand: you shall from this time be

Your master's mistress.

  Oli.   A sister! you are she.

Enter [*Fabian,* with] *Malvolio.*

Duke. Is this the madman?

  Oli.   Ay, my lord, this same. 350

How now, Malvolio?

  Mal.   Madam, you have done me
    wrong,

Notorious wrong.

  Oli.   Have I, Malvolio? No.   355

  Mal. Lady, you have. Pray you peruse that letter.

You must not now deny it is your hand.

361. **in the modesty of honor:** in honest modesty.

362. **lights:** indications.

365. **lighter:** lesser.

367. **suffered:** allowed.

369. **geck and gull:** simpleton and fool.

372. **character:** handwriting.

376-77. **in such forms which here were presupposed/ Upon thee:** in such style as was suggested to you here.

378. **practice:** plot; **shrewdly:** severely; **passed upon:** tricked.

Write from it if you can, in hand or phrase,
Or say 'tis not your seal, not your invention.
You can say none of this. Well, grant it then,   360
And tell me, in the modesty of honor,
Why you have given me such clear lights of favor,
Bade me come smiling and cross-gartered to you,
To put on yellow stockings, and to frown
Upon Sir Toby and the lighter people;   365
And, acting this in an obedient hope,
Why have you suffered me to be imprisoned,
Kept in a dark house, visited by the priest,
And made the most notorious geck and gull
That e'er invention played on? Tell me why.   370

Oli. Alas, Malvolio, this is not my writing,
Though I confess much like the character;
But, out of question, 'tis Maria's hand.
And now I do bethink me, it was she
First told me thou wast mad. Thou camest in smiling, 375
And in such forms which here were presupposed
Upon thee in the letter. Prithee be content.
This practice hath most shrewdly passed upon thee;
But when we know the grounds and authors of it,
Thou shalt be both the plaintiff and the judge   380
Of thine own cause.

Fab.   Good madam, hear me speak,
And let no quarrel, nor no brawl to come,
Taint the condition of this present hour,
Which I have wond'red at. In hope it shall not,   385
Most freely I confess myself and Toby
Set this device against Malvolio here,

388-89. Upon some stubborn and uncourteous parts/ We had conceived against him: because of some rigid and ungracious characteristics of his that we disliked.

390. importance: importunity, persuasion.

396. baffled: made a mock of; see II. v. 158.

409. convents: agrees, suits everyone.

Upon some stubborn and uncourteous parts
We had conceived against him. Maria writ
The letter, at Sir Toby's great importance,   390
In recompense whereof he hath married her.
How with a sportful malice it was followed
May rather pluck on laughter than revenge,
If that the injuries be justly weighed
That have on both sides passed.   395

   Oli. Alas poor fool, how have they baffled thee!

   Clown. Why, "some are born great, some achieve
greatness, and some have greatness thrown upon
them." I was one, sir, in this interlude—one Sir Topas,
sir; but that's all one. "By the Lord, fool, I am not   400
mad!" But do you remember—"Madam, why laugh
you at such a barren rascal? An you smile not, he's
gagged"? And thus the whirligig of time brings in his
revenges.

   Mal. I'll be revenged on the whole pack of you!   405
                                                    [Exit.]

   Oli. He hath been most notoriously abused.

   Duke. Pursue him and entreat him to a peace.
He hath not told us of the captain yet.
When that is known, and golden time convents,
A solemn combination shall be made   410
Of our dear souls. Meantime, sweet sister,
We will not part from hence. Cesario, come—
For so you shall be while you are a man;
But when in other habits you are seen,
Orsino's mistress and his fancy's queen.   415
                         Exeunt [all but the Clown].

Back step.
From Cesare Negri, *Nuove inventioni di balli* (1604).
(See I. iii. 119.)

Clown sings.

When that I was and a little tiny boy,
  With hey, ho, the wind and the rain,
A foolish thing was but a toy,
  For the rain it raineth every day.

But when I came to man's estate,   420
  With hey, ho, the wind and the rain,
'Gainst knaves and thieves men shut their gate,
  For the rain it raineth every day.

But when I came, alas! to wive,
  With hey, ho, the wind and the rain,   425
By swaggering could I never thrive,
  For the rain it raineth every day.

But when I came unto my beds,
  With hey, ho, the wind and the rain,
With tosspots still had drunken heads,   430
  For the rain it raineth every day.

A great while ago the world begun,
  With hey, ho, the wind and the rain;
But that's all one, our play is done,
  And we'll strive to please you every day.   435

                                 [Exit.]

Famous Lines and Phrases

If music be the food of love, play on   [*Orsino*—I. i. 1]

And what should I do in Illyria?   [*Viola*—I. ii. 3]

O, you are sick of self-love, Malvolio, and taste with a distempered appetite.   [*Olivia*—I. v. 92-3]

Make me a willow cabin at your gate
And call upon my soul within the house;
Write loyal cantons of contemned love
And sing them loud even in the dead of night . . .
          [*Viola*—I. v. 273-76]

. . . she bore a mind that envy could not but call fair.
          [*Sebastian*—II. i. 28-9]

O Time, thou must untangle this, not I;
It is too hard a knot for me t'untie!   [*Viola*—II. ii. 40-1]

Not to be abed after midnight is to be up betimes . . .
          [*Toby*—II. iii. 1-2]

[Song]   O mistress mine, where are you roaming . . .
          [*Clown*—II. iii. 39-44, 47-52]

Am not I consanguineous?   [*Toby*—II iii. 77]

Dost thou think, because thou art virtuous, there shall be no
more cakes and ale?   [*Toby*—II. iii. 117-18]

I have no exquisite reason for't, but I have reason good enough.
          [*Andrew*—II. iii. 145-46]

The spinsters and the knitters in the sun,
And the free maids that weave their thread with bones,
Do use to chant it.   [*Orsino*—II. iv. 52-5]

[Song]   Come away, come away, death . . .
                                   [*Clown*—II. iv. 60-76]

She never told her love,
But let concealment, like a worm i' the bud,
Feed on her damask cheek.   [*Viola*—II. iv. 125-27]

. . . like Patience on a monument   [*Viola*—II. iv. 129]

Some are born great, some achieve greatness, and some have
    greatness thrust upon 'em.   [*Malvolio*—II. v. 141-42]

[Song]   When that I was and a little tiny boy . . .
                                   [*Clown*—V. i. 416-35]

The Folger Library

Shakespeare

☐ 66923	ALL'S WELL THAT ENDS WELL $2.95	☐ 73354	A MIDSUMMER NIGHT'S DREAM $3.50
☐ 47711	ANTONY AND CLEOPATRA $3.50	☐ 50814	MUCH ADO ABOUT NOTHING $3.95
☐ 72953	AS YOU LIKE IT $3.50	☐ 50815	OTHELLO $3.95
☐ 73990	COMEDY OF ERRORS $3.50	☐ 53142	RICHARD II $2.95
☐ 49966	CORIOLANUS $3.95	☐ 72656	RICHARD III $3.50
☐ 66925	CYMBELINE $2.95	☐ 72768	ROMEO AND JULIET $3.50
☐ 66922	FOUR COMEDIES $4.95	☐ 66914	PERICLES $2.95
☐ 60105	FOUR TRAGEDIES $4.95	☐ 67047	SHAKESPEARE'S SONNETS $2.95
☐ 72654	HAMLET $3.50	☐ 66926	SHAKESPEARE'S SONNETS AND POEMS $4.95
☐ 73355	HENRY IV, Part I $3.50		
☐ 73909	HENRY IV, Part II $3.50	☐ 74079	TAMING OF THE SHREW $3.50
☐ 72718	HENRY V $3.50	☐ 55178	THE TEMPEST $2.95
☐ 66918	HENRY VI, Part I $2.95	☐ 66935	TIMON OF ATHENS $2.95
☐ 66919	HENRY VI, Part II $2.95		
☐ 47932	HENRY VIII $2.95	☐ 66915	TITUS ANDRONICUS $2.95
☐ 72655	JULIUS CEASAR $3.50	☐ 66916	TROLIUS AND CRESSIDA $2.95
☐ 66920	KING JOHN $2.95		
☐ 72766	KING LEAR $3.50	☐ 66917	THE WINTER'S TALE $2.95
☐ 66921	LOVE'S LOST LABOR $2.95	☐ 72954	TWELFTH NIGHT $3.50
☐ 74394	MACBETH $3.50	☐ 74395	TWO GENTLEMEN OF VERONA $4.95
☐ 49612	MEASURE FOR MEASURE $2.95		
☐ 72767	THE MERCHANT OF VENICE $3.50		
☐ 73143	MERRY WIVES OF WINDSOR $3.50		

WSP

Simon & Schuster Mail Order Dept. FLS
200 Old Tappan Rd., Old Tappan, N.J. 07675

Please send me the books I have checked above. I am enclosing $_____ (please add 75¢ to cover postage and handling for each order. Please add appropriate local sales tax). Send check or money order—no cash or C.O.D.'s please. Allow up to six weeks for delivery. For purchases over $10.00 you may use VISA: card number, expiration date and customer signature must be included.

Name _____

Address _____

City _____ State/Zip _____

VISA Card No. _____ Exp. Date _____

Signature _____

189-09

CLASSICS THAT WILL DELIGHT READERS OF EVERY AGE!

____70136 ADVENTURES OF HUCKLEBERRY FINN Mark Twain $3.95

____70137 ADVENTURES OF TOM SAWYER Mark Twain $3.95

____70466 AND THEN THERE WERE NONE Agatha Christie $4.95

____70761 ANNE FRANK: THE DIARY OF A YOUNG GIRL
Anne Frank $4.95

____70494 CALL OF THE WILD Jack London $3.95

____47369 A CHRISTMAS CAROL Charles Dickens $2.95

____72651 THE GOOD EARTH Pearl S. Buck $4.95

____72652 KON TIKI Thor Heyerdahl $4.95

____46211 LEGEND OF SLEEPY HOLLOW Washington Irving $3.95

____50439 LES MISERABLES Victor Hugo $5.95

____74582 ODYSSEY Walter James Miller and Henry Shefter $4.50

____54311 OEDIPUS THE KING Sophicles $3.95

____70496 PYGMALION George Bernard Shaw $3.95

____74081 THE RED BADGE OF COURAGE Stephen Crane $3.95

____72467 THE SCARLET LETTER Nathaniel Hawthorne $4.95

____69583 A TALE OF TWO CITIES Charles Dickens $4.95

____72653 UTOPIA Sir Thomas More $3.95

WSP

**Simon & Schuster, Mail Order Dept. ECY
200 Old Tappan Rd., Old Tappan, N.J. 07675**

Please send me the books I have checked above. I am enclosing $_____ (please add 75¢ to cover postage and handling for each order. Please add appropriate local sales tax). Send check or money order— no cash or C.O.D.'s please. Allow up to six weeks for delivery. For purchases over $10.00 you may use VISA: card number, expiration date and customer signature must be included.

Name _____

Address _____

City _____ State/Zip _____

VISA Card No. _____ Exp. Date _____

Signature _____ 363-13